COTTON MATHIS

Journey to Memphis

Cecilia Croft Clanton

ISBN: 1984195166
ISBN 13: 9781984195166
Library of Congress Control Number: 2017918874
CreateSpace Independent Publishing Platform
North Charleston, South Carolina

Dedicated with Love to my Husband

Imagine that fate is nothing more than dominoes. Everything in your life, whether it is luck or loss, would depend on being knocked over by the force of the life next to yours. Now imagine it is 1968, and you live in Memphis, Tennessee. You would be unaware that God, in his weariness with America's civil-rights record, had pulled tragedy from his potent portfolio of instructions and handpicked your city as his classroom.

As the Lord peered down on Memphis that spring, he witnessed a city obsessed with garbage and the men who collected it. He seized the opportunity to set fate into motion with a sweeping arc of his exquisite hand.

Providence placed me in Memphis when everything changed. This is a story of chance, invisible connections, gnawing regret, and tender reprieve. I am Cotton Mathis, and this is my story.

Had things gone as planned when I arrived in Memphis—on a bus, in the middle of the night—there wouldn't be much of a story to tell. I was supposed to be there less than a week; now, many years later, I am still trying to unravel what happened to me in Memphis.

Tonight I am thinking of the morning I moved into the white clapboard house in a neighborhood where I clearly did not belong. I see myself unpacking the few clothes I had with me, most of those purchased for me by the FBI. I moved into the bathroom, and there I cut a piece of cardboard and taped it over the top of the mirror so that I could see just enough to shave—but so I couldn't see the upper portion of my face.

I look from my bedroom window now, and I see the rubble of a burned building in the yard and a young boy with thick glasses drop his bike on the sidewalk below and walk up to the charred remains.

Lately the memories are more vivid. Most nights when I sit down at my office desk, after everyone else has long ago surrendered to sleep, it takes me a few minutes to get settled. I have to move the lamp around so the light falls just right on the paper that's rolled into my typewriter; the glass of water has to be placed in a spot so if it spills, it will not ruin the stack of completed pages; and the radio must not be too loud, but not too soft either—just enough melody to lift the loneliness of the late hour. But tonight—tonight the lamp's light falls perfectly on the page, the water is already half drunk, and the radio dial has not been moved from the evening before, so it is perfect, all perfect.

Tonight everything is in its place, and I am ready to tell my story, the story that even after years of writing, and hundreds of stories, is the only one that matters.

PART ONE

In Cotton's Land

CHAPTER ONE

Marianna, Arkansas, 1963

On a Friday just before noon, my brother and I, dog-tired from the Indian-summer heat, made our way through thick woods. For over an hour, I had been out of water, but my brother, still with a half-full canteen, was determined not to leave until he had killed a deer. "By God," he said, "I need to pull the trigger somethin' bad today, and I'm not leavin' until I do, so you just suck it up and keep movin', 'cause I have the keys to the truck."

Brittle branches snapped like breaking bones under my graceless gait, but my brother's steps were silent. He moved as smoke through the forest, with no regard for the well-worn trail, gliding through the trees with the elegance of a spectral figure. But his shadowy outline left something else in its wake, something that was threatening and ominous, because on this September morning in the unseasonable heat, he smoldered with anger over a slight made by his football coach the day before.

"Keep your gun up," he said to me in a low voice. "I mean that. Keep your finger on that trigger. Just 'cause we haven't seen anything, doesn't mean we won't. It's all about the reflexes. Don't forget that."

Together we pushed forward through the woods with no deer in sight and plenty of time to concentrate on one another's deficiencies. "Can't you be quiet? Can't you do anything right?" he asked.

Even under the canopy of ancient oaks, the sun streamed through the trees enough to make me sweat. My gun slipped in my hand, and my boots filled with moisture. I didn't even care about being quiet; I just wanted this hunt to be over.

My brother growled under his breath—unintelligible mutterings, threats punctuated with jabs of his rifle against tree trunks in his path. I was right about the smoke and the foreboding. This was an early, all-too-familiar sign of heated frustration boiling somewhere deep inside of him. The football coach was now in his head, repeating over and over and over the insult from yesterday. Now my brother was talking out loud to the coach: "Kiss my ass, you fat slob. You'll never be anything but a high-school coach in Arkansas, and I am going to play for the University of Alabama. See ya, asshole."

He became my dangerous companion in the thick of a mental game of looking for an appropriate target; anyone with a heartbeat, any warm-blooded body would do. I walked and watched and waited for the moment when he would decide his strategy and strike in my direction with every last kernel, everything that had been stored and suppressed.

And then it happened.

"You gettin' hungry, Chippie?" he sneered and chugged from his canteen, throwing a few peanuts into his mouth without offering me a sip or even a handful of salty shells to suck on. I didn't respond. "Huh? You hungry? Chippie?"

Chippie. It was his favorite nickname for me, a constant reminder of the time he had knocked a large chip out of my front tooth after I had tattled on him. I was seven, and he, ten. Now every time he said the word, I felt in my mouth for the chipped tooth. I hated the name.

Still, I didn't respond, just as I had not responded to him all morning.

"That's a question, Chippie," he growled, the words like the jabs of his gun on the tree trunks. "Are. You. Hungry?"

Finally, I snapped under the weight of my silence. "Yes. You know I'm hungry. I told you that this morning, but you wouldn't let me have breakfast. You said there wasn't time and that you had something in the truck for us to eat on the way…I shouldn't have believed you. You always take care of yourself and to hell with everyone else," I said.

My brother smirked and chucked another handful of peanuts into his mouth, licked his lips, and dug around the inside of his mouth with his finger, looking for soppy crumbs.

"You know," he said, leaning in, "whenever I come out here alone, I get a good shot in no time. I mean, like, always. Never fails. Quick."

He cocked his head to the left and opened his mouth wide. I watched as he went deeper and deeper, until even his knuckles were gone, then he squinted and furrowed his brow and really focused, and he pulled out a rigid, round chuck of peanut and held it in front of his face. He smiled and stuck it back in his mouth, not even bothering to chew.

"It's those clumsy feet of yours," he said. "That's it; you make too much damn noise. I keep tellin' you, man, you gotta be soft and easy; you gotta stop snapping shit in half and crunching everything you see. You gotta move deep into the forest floor, not on top of it."

Now he set the game in motion. "I'll tell you what," he said with a grin that taunted. "If you can for once be quiet, I mean really quiet like me, I'll bet we'll spot something. If we do, and I get a good clear shot and I nail it—like right between the eyes—I nail that sucker good, then I'll buy you lunch at Booker's. You can have anything you want. I'll buy."

"Whatcha think, Chippie? Sound good? You hungry?"

I looked at the ground and did not respond.

"I'll take that as a 'yes, man,'" he cackled. "Quiet now, remember."

We continued through a thicket of sweet gum trees toward a distant clearing. I closed my eyes to imagine I was floating, but still there was the noise of leaves and sticks crunching under the sole of my shoes. And even with my eyes closed, I could feel the pressure coming from my brother's clenched jaw. He stopped in the clearing, shielded his eyes with a sweaty palm, and looked from left to right. The sun burned, he was out of water, and I was hopeless. He sighed and took a deep breath. "Screw it; come on," he said. "Let's go back. There is nothing goin' on here today. I wanna a nap before football practice, so I can keep that coach off my ass. I gotta look sharp; the Alabama scouts are gonna be here in a few days."

We headed in the direction of the shiny new truck he had purchased in a sweetheart deal from a car dealer who had graduated from one of the several colleges that were courting my brother at the time. "After I get my scholarship, you'll have to hunt alone, Chippie. Try not to get yourself killed. I've taught you everything I know."

He sensed I wasn't there; I was dreaming about floating, about the joy of hunting alone, and he slapped me on the back of the head to reinforce it all. I tried to swat him away, but in a second, he was gone, two steps ahead of me, making no sound, leaving all the branches and twigs for me to trample.

We walked another half mile. I was hungry and thirsty and sopping in sweat. Then, with his steady gaze my brother spotted something and stopped dead in his tracks, his eyes wide and his head cocked, ears twitching like an animal.

Though I hadn't said a word for over an hour, he reached back to motion me to be quiet, his finger pointed down at my feet. There were crackling, shuffling sounds. The birds and the ruffling leaves became hushed. Dipping into deep shadows of hardwood trees, we were bewildered as we studied the landscape. The afternoon sun streaming through the leaves gave the inexplicable sound a column of protection from our slowly adapting sight, but when the focus finally set, we stood rigid in awe as a twelve-point buck approached from seventy-five yards away, unaware that he was being watched. The buck paused to graze in an open meadow. My brother was in front of me, so I waited as he set the scope on his 30.06 rifle, braced his body, and readied to take the shot.

I held my breath so as not to make a sound as he dropped the gun a bit and locked eyes with the deer. It was a contest of wills. The mighty buck had escaped death long enough to branch a magnificent crown of honor. He had no intention of meeting death with a whimper. He held his ground—not a twitch, not a blink.

But my brother did something I had never seen him do before. He hesitated. He never pulled the trigger, and the buck soared over a barbed wire fence and looked back to mock us. His white tail vanished into the woods. My panicked older brother, who had taught me everything, was now sniffling with shame.

"It's too damn hot out here," he said, sheepish. "My finger, it just slipped off the trigger."

He looked in my direction, but I didn't look back at him. I didn't say a word. I looked down and held my breath.

And then, after a long silence, my strong and powerful brother raised my chin with his index finger, looked me dead in the eyes, and said in a whisper like I had never heard from him, "Don't ever tell anyone. *Please.*"

When we got back to the truck, I opened the door, and once inside, I still didn't dare speak. My brother revved the engine and slammed his foot on the accelerator, with dust flying as we barreled down the river road toward Booker's place.

"You gonna do what I asked?" he said finally. "You gonna keep this between us…huh? Answer me." I nodded my head and looked down the road.

"You better not say anything, damn you. I can't have anything make me look weak. I gotta have that scholarship.

Nobody's ever graduated from college in our family. It is my only chance to get outta this hellhole," he said.

I had never understood why he hated eastern Arkansas. The hardwood forests we grew up in were filled with giant oaks and beautiful flowering dogwoods in their understory. The farmland was the envy of the world, with its flat, black earth so fertile the cotton practically sprang from it. When it rained, there was a fresh smell from that dirt, so earthy it was primordial. I would never live anywhere else. Our mother loved it here too.

My favorite memory was of her standing on the back porch and watching the sun go down in the afternoons with her hand placed on my shoulder. The mingled, majestic lights of pink and golden washed over our hardships like a lather of hope. It had been our special time of day together, from the time I was just a small boy.

"I don't know why I couldn't pull the trigger," my brother blurted out, interrupting my thoughts.

I felt him looking at me, searching for any indication that I understood what he had admitted. From the corner of my eye, I watched him as he watched me from the corner of his, but for once I didn't give myself away to him. I sat still, I kept quiet, and I knew I could win this one if I just didn't fold.

A moment passed before he continued, "I just hope it doesn't happen when I've got a football in my hand. Everything depends on it. Don't you mess this up for me, and I mean it! You won't just have a chip in your tooth. You won't have any teeth left."

With that, he pressed harder on the accelerator, and I watched as we passed Booker's place, the smell of barbecue swirling through the air.

"What about my lunch?" I said and watched Booker's place get smaller and smaller through the rearview mirror. "It was a game, and I won it."

My brother slammed on the brakes, and the truck halted dead in the middle of the road. The driver behind us honked and glared as he went around us.

"You didn't win," he said, his eyes wide and incredulous. "I swear, sometimes you say shit that is so stupid."

I looked right at him, and he looked back at me. From behind us, cars honked, sped by, and tossed out obscene gestures.

"You said it was my fault...I was too loud," I said and shook a bit but became more assertive with every syllable. "You told me to be quiet. You said if I was quiet, we'd see something, and we did. We saw a buck. You coulda shot it; he was right there in front of you."

My brother's response was a nervous laugh, like he'd stumbled in on the tail of a joke he didn't understand but laughed just to be part of the crowd. Then he started to speak; his neck arched forward, and the skin around his mouth stretched. But nothing came out, not a phrase or a word or a noise—or anything that even came close to flirting with a sound.

I was right, and he knew it, and for the first and only time in his life, in our history, he didn't push back. He just sat there, behind the wheel of his shiny new truck, in the middle of a road nestled deep in the delta, next to me, his brother, the target of anything and everything he wanted to punish, the mirror he used to somehow convince himself that he was really, truly worth something.

In that moment, he was stumped; I had stumped him. The adrenaline was so fierce, so palpable, that I capitalized on the silence and dug deeper.

"You lost the game," I said. "You said you would get him and get him good. You had a clear shot. You coulda gotten him right between the eyes, just like you said, but you didn't, did you?"

I gulped and smiled and waited for the response, but remarkably, there wasn't one.

"It's your loss, and it's my win. I win. I'm hungry. So turn around and go back to Booker's. I'm hungry, and you're buying. Winners get to eat whatever they want; you should know that better than anybody."

From the middle of the road, my brother turned the truck around when the traffic cleared, and we headed for Booker's place and my lunch.

CHAPTER TWO

When we arrived at the home of Booker and Sallie Benton, the smoke from the barbecue pit filled the backyard. There were always people milling around at the Bentons', hunters picking up their processed deer meat, white families buying barbecue and home-baked fruit pies for dinner, or the church gospel choir who used the Bentons' place to practice each week.

Booker was enormous, especially muscular in his neck and arms. His skin was as dark as the sumptuous soil he farmed. It was as if he and the earth on which he stood were one and the same. Miss Sallie was small, lean, and energetic. She walked on tiptoes as she twirled through her daily life with the grace of a ballerina and the joy of a child. Each morning she pinned back her long hair and wore one of her well-fitting dresses, sewn on her ancient Singer machine.

Standing against Booker's leg was his prized yellow Labrador hunting dog, Dewdrop. Booker had found him early one morning, an abandoned pup on the roadside in the wet grass. Booker said it was as if the dog had dropped from the sky just like the dew at daybreak, so he was christened Dewdrop.

The dog broke from Booker and raced for me; he leapt into my arms and, on his hind legs, licked my face like a wash towel.

"You boys doin' okay? You get a deer out there?" Booker asked.

"No, sir, didn't even see one." My brother looked at me and the dog with a glare and said, "Could we get a couple of sandwiches and slaw from you?"

I returned my brother's glare and said, "I'll take two barbecues, so make that three, would you, Booker?" I felt even more emboldened with the dog hugging me.

"Sure, we'll have 'em ready in no time," Booker said and pulled the dog from me. "Dew's always so glad to see you. He just tryin' to tell you he will never forget you saved his life and mine, and Sallie never gonna forget it either. You can fear no man as long as I'm alive, because I'll take care of you just like you took care of Dew. If you hadn't come along, I would've died right there next to that dog."

I raised both hands to let Booker know the many times he had thanked me were more than enough. My brother did not like to be reminded of this incident, but it came up around town pretty often.

Torrential downpours had hit this delta region last November, and creeks that had never flooded became raging rivers of tree limbs, old tires, and farm equipment. With the ground so saturated, Booker's hogpen had collapsed and his entire herd of swine had escaped, but Dewdrop alerted the family in the early-morning hours. Booker and Dew set out at dawn to round up the hogs and got most of them home, but three piglets slipped into a creek at the back of the property. Normally three feet deep, the creek was now seven feet and deadly, especially for Booker, who couldn't swim. Dew went in after the pigs and was knocked underwater by a huge forked limb that had become lodged in debris. The dog clung to it, his head barely out of the freezing water.

Booker was terrified, but he waded in after Dew and was frozen with such fear he could not move toward the dog or the shore; this man who feared no one was paralyzed in waist-deep water, with the outside temperature hovering at thirty-four degrees.

For me that day was just a simple as a lucky break. Concerned about our deer stands and hunting camp, I had decided to throw on my waders and brave the pouring rain and cold. When I came upon them, Dew was seconds from drowning, and Booker was crying with shame that he could not reach him. I threw Booker a line and swam in to rescue Dewdrop from the tree. He wrapped his front legs around me, and we made it out together. The doctor said both of them were mere minutes from dying of hypothermia, but I just had done what anyone lucky enough to come across them that day would have done.

Booker turned his attention to my brother and asked, "How is your senior season lookin'? How many colleges you been talkin' to?"

"Six right now," my brother answered, "but I tell you the truth, man, the only one I care about is Alabama. I want to play for Bear Bryant."

"Bear Bryant? Now there's an Arkansas boy who has done good. What you want to study?" Booker asked.

"Engineering. I want to live in Chicago someday and build skyscrapers," my brother said.

I moved away from them and next to the truck, so there would be no chance my brother would get out of paying for my lunch. Booker looked my way and said, "Hey, why you keep your hand in your pockets all the time? You can't eat like that. Get over here and sit down with us."

Dew and I walked to the picnic table, and Booker smiled at me as he set the two sandwiches in front of me and asked, "Aren't you proud of your brother? Everyone in town is talking about him."

When I responded with a less-than-convincing nod, my brother said to Booker, "You know he doesn't say much. He's a writer. He's always typing alone back there in his room. God knows what he is writing about; I'm afraid to ask." Both of them laughed, and Booker gave me an affectionate pat on the back as he turned to tend the pit.

They were both right. I kept my hands in my pockets because there was always a key there, and I liked the feel of it in my hand, and I didn't say much because my brother talked for me. My parents had worried when, at two years old, I wasn't putting sentences together. The doctor said I was lazy and just allowed my brother to speak for me. I had grown tired of the sound of his voice.

I had always wanted to be a writer, and though I enjoyed sports, I spent a good amount of time in our local library when I was growing up. The lady who worked there would call my mother when new adventure books arrived, so I could be the first to read them. *The Hardy Boys* and the books of Jack London transported me to places I knew I had little chance to see, but I relished my visits in those exciting pages.

As a boy hunting with my brother, I imagined us as great Indian warriors and wrote short stories about our exploits in the forest during camping trips under starless summer nights by the L'Anguille River. I wrote down each story by hand and tucked them all into a fancy box that belonged to my mother before she died of cervical cancer in 1960. It was the key to that box that I kept in my pocket. Stored there was a photograph of her when she was a girl and another of my parents on the day they were married. My favorite was a picture of my mother standing by a car, with my brother and me perched above the headlights. It was the only new car our family ever owned, and my proud mother had a broad smile.

Our father was a welder in the auto-parts plant; he repaired farm equipment on the side. Though he never spoke of the war or the gash-like scar over his right eye, he was a World War II veteran who had served two tours in Europe. From Friday afternoon until Sunday evening, he drank straight bourbon with ice, never allowing the rhythm of our family life to interrupt him.

Not a mean drunk, he snoozed on the couch and laughed at private jokes he told himself. Sometimes as I passed through the den, he would grab my arm and stare at me as if I, too, were privileged to share the joke, as his eyes welled with tears and laughter.

While I resented our father's drinking, my brother would patiently sit next to him on the couch and hold his hand. Their conversations were low and serious. I never knew what they spoke about, but their talks always ended with my father promising to do better.

Our rental rested on the imaginary line that divided the white and black neighborhoods of our community. The houses were all the same: six steps led up to a front porch; inside, a parlor room was on the left, with a dining room on the right. To the rear were the kitchen and two bedrooms. The bathroom was in the hallway. Each house had a faded-white-wood exterior. The window shutters, instead of protecting the privacy of the owner, revealed their occupant's status. Nondescript green, black, or gray shutters hung on the houses of the white residents. But on the black neighbors' side, shades of pink, purple, red, and orange burst from the window frames like summer zinnias planted in a garden row.

Music drifted from the black side, played from porch radios or by the singing of busy mothers in their kitchens, while from our white side, there was only a ticking tedium. On Saturdays I cherished my solitary walk downtown to shop from the detailed list my mother had assigned me. If I was quiet, I could hear gospel, blues, and jazz spinning in the air, coming together and wrapping me like a hand-knitted sweater.

Black people and white people lived separate lives in those days, and I never gave that much thought as we all went about our daily duties with benign indifference in our divided schools, grocery stores, and movie theaters. But, when the cancer made my mother too sick to rise from bed in the mornings, it was the black ladies who lived nearby who brought us food and helped her to the lavatory, and I never forgot their kindness.

I had no singular childhood memories of my own because my brother was the source of all sunlight for our family. He was popular and blindingly handsome. He was the local football hero for blacks and whites alike. He was never alone; a laughing, faithful crowd followed him everywhere. He had a talent for connecting things: people with each other, a flying football with his hand, and our family with respectability.

My game was baseball. I loved baseball almost as much as hunting, and by my sophomore year, I was the starting varsity catcher. The posters of the great Tim McCarver, the Memphis-born Cardinals catcher, wallpapered my bedroom.

My father never once attended my baseball games. He hated the game, and one afternoon in my junior year, as I listened in my room to a Cardinals game on the radio, he burst in and took my bat and smashed the radio into small pieces. I quit baseball for good the next day.

He did, however, attend every one of my brother's football games. According to him, football was the sport of real men.

Excitement at the prospect of my brother's senior season surrounded the community, our school, and particularly my family. With my brother in his last season and his third as our starting quarterback, the crowds grew larger and larger. An unbroken line of black neighbors viewed the game from behind the fence that surrounded the stadium. Flags of gold and black, the school colors, flapped overhead in the windy but warm weather.

Last week's game had been flawless. We won by twenty-one points, and there was little fear of this less-talented opponent. I never enjoyed the games because my time was spent looking over my shoulder to see if our father had stumbled into the stadium. On that night, as always, sitting next to me were my best friends, Froggie and Timbo. Froggie was lanky, blond, and awkward in his gait, while Timbo exuded the easy confidence of being born into a wealthy and prominent family.

Many of our conversations were about the mysteries of the female mind. "Hey, you could probably see the game better if you come sit with us," Froggie yelled out, as three girls from our class walked by together. They giggled among themselves and waved but showed no interest in joining us.

Froggie interrupted my thoughts and said, "Look, those must be the scouts from Alabama. Did your brother know they were comin' tonight?"

"Yeah," I answered. "They've been expected since last week. Too bad they didn't get here for the last game."

The crowd erupted as the referee yelled, "Touchdown!" My brother had found his favorite receiver, and we were on the boards. I said a silent prayer of thanks as people came by and slapped me on the back.

With the extra point kicked, I resumed my watch over the stadium entrance, and there, next to the concession stand, stood my father with his hand resting on the counter. I moved to stand at the end of the bleachers and hoped my drunken dad wouldn't cause a scene.

"Don't worry about it. Nobody is paying attention to him. They're all looking at your brother," said Timbo.

On our next possession, right after the ball was snapped, even from where I stood, I spotted confusion on my brother's face as he hesitated, with the ball cocked in the air. Before he could gather himself and release it, he was tackled.

"What was *that?*" Froggie said with his palms in the air. "He was wide open. Something must have happened we couldn't see."

But I knew better. Something had been roiling inside my brother's head for days, and it erupted when he ran to the bench and banged his helmet against it.

The rest of the game, he never connected for an appreciable pass. My father left the bleachers weeping, and people in the stands were uncomfortable with his emotional outburst. The scouts left early in the fourth quarter. We lost the game fourteen to seven.

Losses piled up week after week, and we finished the season with a miserable three wins and seven losses. There would be no scholarship.

The day after my brother graduated from high school, he enlisted in the army. "It's not football, Chippie, but at least they'll pay for my college. I gotta get out of here, and maybe I can distinguish myself in the service. Vietnam can't be much worse than watching Alabama on television and not being on the field," he said on the day he left for basic training. "I don't know what you gonna do about Daddy. Just try to be patient with him."

I answered my brother with a nod, but I had no idea what to do about our father either. The prospect of three years alone with him was not something I relished.

"I've got a feelin' you're gonna have a bunch of medals when you come home," I said to him before he boarded the troop bus. "You're just that kinda guy. We'll be rooting for you." I hugged him tighter than I ever had and thought how gratified our mother would have been to see him in uniform.

I missed my brother much more than I ever imagined. For days after his departure, I refused to look into a mirror, afraid there would be nothing looking back at me. When I finally caught a glimpse of myself in a store window, I recoiled from the lack of recognition of my own face. After he was gone, I realized that for all my life, I had not just wanted to be more like him, I wanted to *be* him. Even with this disappointment, his life would always be better than my own; I was resigned to that.

CHAPTER THREE

My final years of high school passed in a blink, and after graduation I lucked upon a job driving a tractor on the Chandler family farm. Though I still lived at home, I moved into young-adult life with my friends and even began to date a little. My father was so determined to make my brother proud of him; he joined Alcoholics Anonymous, and at the top of the daily letters he wrote to him in Vietnam, he logged "364," "365," "366," "367," and so on, to record the number of his sober days. I was proud of him for the first time in my life.

Resentment over the Vietnam War raged in the country, with violent protests on college campuses and in large cities. Every eighteen-year-old male in the country nervously watched the nightly news reports, wondering if he would be the next called into service. Before I could give much thought to the idea of being drafted, Timbo's father, the state senator, handed me a set of National Guard admission papers to sign. National Guard enlistments were treasures often doled out by influential men to keep their family and friends out of Vietnam.

As predicted, my brother excelled in the army and spoke in his letters about making the military his career. Even half a world away, he knew that Alabama finished this 1966 season undefeated and won the Sugar Bowl. It would have been his junior year in college, and I knew the loss of his scholarship still stung.

On a brilliant, cloudless Sunday, Froggie, Timbo, and I hurtled down the river road in Froggie's worn, blue truck, on the way to a fishing trip and a covert mission. The three of us sang at the top of our lungs, with fists held to our mouths for microphones, and belted out our favorite new Temptations song, "Ain't Too Proud to Beg."

"Shut up, man," Froggie said and looked over me to Timbo. "You can't sing a lick. You can't do anything right, man." Froggie and I roared with laughter.

"What have you got to say for yourself? The only reason your ass is still in the National Guard is 'cause your daddy is a big shot. Lucky you, man, 'cause if I blew up a barn with a grenade launcher, my ass would be in Vietnam. You ain't ever gonna live this one down, man."

Timbo was fuming, with his arms crossed at his waist, when the truck came to a stop. "Don't worry; your dad is leaving for the legislature in Little Rock in the morning, and we've kept ya hidden so far," I said. "This'll blow over by the time he comes back home. Let's go fish until dark, and then we can go to Booker's for supper."

I would never admit it to them, but I was I so grateful the three of us had stayed close to home after graduation. I enjoyed my work on the Chandler farm, Froggie had taken a job in the auto-parts plant, and Timbo was attending the junior college in Helena and would eventually work in his father's insurance business. I sat alone in Froggie's truck for a moment, with the fishing worms wiggling in my hand, and enjoyed this escapade of our elusive youth.

There is a sweet softness to the moments before everything changes. You can still dance in the kitchen, sing to the radio, or howl at the moon. But then the broom of fate sweeps you in a dustpan and dumps you into the garbage bin your life becomes. This was one of those moments.

We unloaded our gear on the levee and headed for our fishing hole. "Do you hear that?" I asked. "Someone's callin' us from the river road. Be still."

"Oh, shit, it's probably my dad," whispered Timbo.

"Stay here, let me get a look." Froggie eased to the top of the ridge and looked down. "Yep, it's your old man, Timbo, and he looks mad. How the hell did he find us?"

Timbo's father slammed the door of his truck at the bottom of the levee and, with his long legs, bounded up to the top. Dread washed over me. Through the years I had heard him tear into Timbo at the slightest provocation. He was serious, successful, and impatient. And he was huge. His hands were so large; he often palmed a basketball to keep it away from us in our pick-up games in his driveway. He always won.

When he reached the top, Froggie and I nervously looked toward Timbo, but instead, he went right to me and stood looking down with a knitted brow. He touched my shoulder. "Son, you need to get home right now. Your dad needs you. You boys load up and take him, and I'll see you two back at my house. Now go on."

"What's the matter? Is he drunk? I *don't care*. I am goin' fishin'. I'm sick of him; I hate him. He can't do anything right." I tossed my tackle box to the ground.

But Timbo's father just headed back down the levee and didn't say a word.

Froggie picked up the tackle and said, "Come on now, they ain't bitin' today anyway."

When we reached the house, a dark-blue sedan with Tennessee license plates sat in the driveway behind my father's vehicle. "What the hell is going on?" I muttered as I retrieved my fishing gear from the back and waved to my friends.

No lights illuminated the room when I entered from the blinding sun of a perfect afternoon. My father sat on the same couch where he had slept on so many drunken nights. He was now between an overweight minister whose collar strained in the afternoon heat, and whose face was swollen and damp, and a uniformed man who, by contrast, appeared to have just stepped from the shower and walked into newly pressed clothes.

"It's your brother. He's dead," my father blurted out and began to wail like a wounded animal. I stood stock-still, showing no emotion, unable to accept that the sun had set on our family and it would never be morning again. I remembered the words said about my father on the levee and began to cry; I knelt next to him.

The officer reached for me. "Son, you will be getting more information from your brother's commanding officers in a week or so. We're here to make sure his remains get home and help you with the arrangements. We'll stay with you until the funeral is over and get the benefits your family is due processed as soon as possible."

His words ran together and spilled out like an overturned bowl of soup on the counter, leaving an unrecognizable mess all around.

"Let's get my dad to bed; could you just help me with that?" We both lifted his limp body from the couch, and the officer helped him take off his boots as I turned back the covers.

Later in the living room, I demanded an answer from both men. "Why? What did he die for? Tell me—*tell* me *now*—what did he die for?"

"Son," the minister struggled to get his breath against his weight and the heat, "every time I deliver this news, that's the one question the family always asks and the one that has no answer. Let's bow our heads now and go to the Lord, the only answer to every question."

I took the man's Bible from his fat hands and threw it across the room with a force so strong that it tore the wallpaper from the living room wall, and I left them praying as I retraced the steps I once took to town on errands for my mother.

The whole community turned out for the funeral. The streets were lined with flags, and patriotic music from the high-school band accompanied my brother's casket as his former football-team members lifted it up the church steps. Ministers from the Baptist, Methodist, and Presbyterian churches spoke on my family's behalf. Afterward, at a reception at Timbo's enormous, white-columned home, food filled every table in the living area of the house, and children ran and played on the front lawn under the towering oak trees.

When the letter arrived, it was addressed to my father, and he left it open on the dining-room table.

"Your son was outstanding in every way," the commanding officer wrote. "He volunteered for this war when many men in America are turning their backs on the military. He was number one in his class during basic training. When he got to Vietnam, he distinguished himself as an enthusiastic and committed soldier."

Another, wrinkled letter from my brother's platoon leader, written on worn paper, was in the envelope. "Cpl. Mathis and the men under his command entered an abandoned enemy encampment. He covered for his men as they entered the tents left behind. They were attacked by a sniper in the surrounding jungle. Cpl. Mathis was unable to get a shot off, and we think his gun must have jammed or slipped from his hand. He was mortally wounded."

From the kitchen I heard the drunken, slurred voice of my father. "He could have been Bear Bryant's best quarterback. Why couldn't the scouts see it? Everyone knew it. If he had got that scholarship, he'd still be here."

"Go sleep it off, Dad," I said.

"You'll never be like him," he said. "You and those huntin' stories you write. What good is that gonna do anybody? Your mother, now your brother, and I'm stuck here with you. You're never gonna amount to anything."

That was enough. The pent-up feelings and neglect I had endured for nineteen years erupted with the closed fist that I used to knock my father to the ground. He grabbed his jaw and writhed on the floor. "He was a *coward*," I shouted. "Do you hear me—a coward. Now. Get. In. The. Bed."

He crawled to his bedroom. He was my responsibility, and the weight of that felt as heavy and unwanted as the death of my brother. How would I ever keep him from drinking with the reason for his sobriety gone?

To assuage my guilt, I went to the kitchen and cranked the can opener over the top of his favorite tomato soup. I never spent much time in the kitchen, but there was comfort in doing something so normal and mundane, and as I stood at the stove, I tried to concentrate on nothing but the soup. I set the soup on the counter to cool.

When the gunshot fired, I first looked out the window to locate the direction of the blast. My comprehension was in slow motion as it registered the sound had come from my father's bedroom.

By the time I got there, he was dead, with a bullet to the brain. He held pictures of my mother and brother in his hand. I gently removed them and wiped the blood from their faces with the kitchen towel I still held.

We buried my father next to my mother and brother. My entire family was now gone.

At the funeral, after I had shaken the hand of everyone I knew and many more that I did not, I returned to my family home.

Once alone in the kitchen, I went to the drawer for the hammer my father kept there. I went into the living room, and then the bathroom, my parents' room, and finally my own, and I smashed every mirror in the house into shiny dust on the floor. It was not enough to break the glass; I pulverized each piece of it. It took over an hour to sweep the fine powder into a cardboard box. I took the box to the garbage and happened to get there as the trash collector was walking down our broken concrete driveway.

"We're real sorry about your brother, son," he said. "I never did see no one who could make a ball spin like he could." I handed him the box of disintegrated mirrors, walked back to the house, and slammed the door.

The next morning, I shaved in front of the wavy image of myself reflected in the kitchen window.

I locked the doors and answered none of the knocks of my childhood friends, the ministers, or the well-meaning. Late in the afternoons each day, food began to appear at the front door, wrapped in foil and red-checked napkins. It was placed there by the same black ladies who had taken care of my mother and who lived across the imaginary racial line of our neighborhood.

CHAPTER FOUR

Three weeks after my father's death, I had come to dread the night. When the sun dropped into the horizon's envelope, it delivered me into a pit of guilt and shame. After dinner one evening, I sat in front of my typewriter, hoping to distract myself by starting to write a hunting story I had thought about for days. I was ready to put words on paper, to write anything that was not sad and to remember my youth—when my brother and I thought we had ownership of the woods around us and every creature, plant, and tree that resided there. I felt my mood lift as my fingers touched the keys, but when I acted on my reflex to type, I didn't have the strength to make the hammer strike the ribbon of ink to leave an impression on the paper. I was powerless, and after a half hour, when I took my hands away from the machine, they were frozen in a clawlike position, just as if they were still on the typewriter in the position of the key I wanted them to punch. I collapsed on top of the machine, shedding the first tears I had cried since that day on the ridge when everything was lost. I had no family, I had no face in the mirror, and I had no writing voice.

I ripped a jacket from the back of my chair, slammed the kitchen door so hard that it rattled on its hinges, and headed through the backyard into the night for the two-mile walk to the cemetery and the source of my suffering. Had I paid attention at all that day, I would have known there were tornado warnings in the area, and heavy rains predicted throughout the night. The rain was coming down hard by the time I reached the graves, but still I lay across them and cried more than I had ever cried and begged what was left of these three souls to take me where they had gone. I lay there for over an hour, praying the rain would wash me away into the culverts and down into the sewer, and out to the river, and down the Mississippi all the way to New Orleans and past Bourbon Street, into the Gulf and oblivion.

I heard my name called in the rain and the darkness but refused to answer, and when the source of the calling found me, there was a muscular tug on my jacket. Booker and Dew stood over me in the driving rain. "Your kitchen door was wide open, and your truck was still in the driveway. It didn't take me long to figure out where you'd gone."

Booker gathered me up in his enormous arms and held me tight to his chest. My tears and the gulping for air made me so weak I could only surrender to his strength. I tried to speak and was incapable of making a sound—not a whimper or a whine or a moan.

Days later in the medical clinic, the doctor said the cascade of trauma had caused spontaneous mutism, and no one should pressure me to speak.

"His voice may fully recover with time, or he may never make another sound," he told Booker and Sallie while I waited for them in the car. "His chances are fifty-fifty, and that depends on his motivation."

On the way home, Sallie said, "Now don't you worry yourself; the doctor feels like your voice will come back just fine." I had no reason to care; my brother, my parents, and my stories were gone. There was nothing left for me to say.

When Booker took me to Miss Sallie that night, she fed me broth while sitting next to me on the bed and singing "Sweet Chariot"; she hummed it in a soft voice. "Now let's eat up," she said, never looking at me directly and so giving me the luxury of not having to return her gaze. "You need your stren'th to move forward, and we gonna move forward, 'cause movin' back hurts too much."

For days I lay in bed with Dew next to me, his soft body against mine, and at night when we slept, his head rested on my chest. "You two doin' all right?" Miss Sallie asked when she checked on us and brought us food throughout the day. Once I was able to stand and eat on my own, she said, "I think it's time you and Dew helped me in the garden. Why don't you put on your jeans, and we'll go weed for a while."

When I rose from the bed, I noticed for the first time that the room where I rested was filled with photographs of high-school memories much like my own. There were pictures of football games, smiling groups of girls and cheerleaders. I picked up the photograph of a girl in her senior-graduation cap and gown.

"That was our daughter; she was about your age," Miss Sallie said. "She was killed in a car accident on her way back to Detroit. She and her new husband worked in the

Ford manufacturing plant; they both died. I wish you had a chance to know her."

But Sallie and I both knew that would not have happened, even in this small town of six thousand people, with our numbers about evenly divided between white and black. Her daughter and I would never have crossed paths because we traversed different roads within the same universe. I hugged Miss Sallie hard, and we sat on the bed and cried together for a few moments; then she, Dew, and I went out into their world, into the garden, where the tomatoes were ripe and ready to pick, the squash was bright yellow against the black earth, the chickens scratched in the yard, and the weeds awaited us. The fresh air lifted me, and I took a long breath into my stomach and released it slowly from my mouth, and I knew for the first time what healing felt like.

On my first Thursday with the Bentons and every subsequent one, their son Clyde came to help slaughter the hogs and prepare the meat for weekend sales. From the first time I met Clyde, it was obvious he was not happy about my presence but tolerated my showing lame magic tricks to his four-year-old daughter, Olivia; I looked forward to her visits.

One interesting aspect of being mute was that people often thought I was deaf too. From the kitchen where Olivia played, I heard a heated conversation between Clyde and his mother on the front porch.

"Mother, that white man is gonna get you and Daddy shot. You gotta get him out of here. You know how people are. There are gonna be white people and black people who don't like the idea of him being here. You know that."

"Clyde, now you listen to me, and you listen to me good," his mother answered, "that white man didn't just save that dog, he saved your daddy too. We gonna do whatever it takes to help him, and the Lord will protect us. Now, I don't want to hear another word about it."

After Clyde left later that afternoon, the smell of the slaughtered hogs on the grill stagnated throughout the house. Booker and Miss Sallie appeared in the doorway of my room, both wearing white aprons covered in blood. "You'll stay here until you're better," Booker said, "no matter how long it takes. I spoke with Mr. Chandler, and he said your job is waitin' for you when you feel like comin' back to the farm."

I mouthed the words, "Thank you," but Booker put his hand up to let me know it was not necessary. My days with Booker and Miss Sallie became routine, with early mornings spent in the vegetable garden and afternoons in piloting Booker's ancient tractor. We fed the livestock and prepared the weekend barbecue in silence. We ate dinner with the television filling the vacuum of quiet.

I counted the days until Thursdays when Clyde brought Olivia, who replenished the rooms with her laughter and who became comfortable with me, a white man living with her grandparents. My silence was another thing. Finally, she could no longer stand the quiet.

"Why can't you talk? What's the matter with you?" she said. "My daddy says you are just stupid, and my daddy is smart, so he knows. Do you have cotton in your mouth? I am just going to start calling you Cotton; that's a good name for you, Cotton."

Olivia's demands hung in the air, and the three adults looked at me in a way so that she knew she had been rude, and she began to cry. Before the tears reached her cheeks, I scooped her up and swung her around the room. I grabbed the notepad and pen Miss Sallie kept by the telephone and wrote, "Thank you, Olivia; I like the name Cotton." Clyde read the note to her, and she responded by grabbing my legs and then danced her way out into the front yard.

The name worked for me. I would never be the person I had been before, and Olivia's innocence gave me a name to prompt the six months of silent healing space I enjoyed with the Bentons and Dew. My speech made a gradual return, and I practiced twice weekly with a therapist, who helped me regain my verbal skills. The time finally came for me to move on. I would miss the Bentons and Dew, but all of us knew my life resided on the other side of the invisible racial line.

I moved back into my family home, with plans to paint and repair it in my spare time. The first item on my renovation list was a mirror for the bathroom. The day I installed it, I stood there for a long time and said over and over to my reflection, "I am Cotton Mathis, I am Cotton Mathis, I am Cotton Mathis. I am Cotton Mathis," in my slow, stilted voice that still had not completely returned to normal.

It didn't work. I still saw the faces of my mother, brother, and father staring back at me. I could no more convince myself they were not there anymore than I could convince myself that my arms and legs were not attached to my body. I cut a piece of cardboard and placed it over the top of the mirror, leaving just enough space so that I could see to shave in the morning but I would not have to look myself in the eyes.

My return to work at the Chandler farm fell during the busiest part of the harvest season. The physical work and easy camaraderie with my coworkers were medicinal in their healing.

As the days passed, I knew in time I would speak in full again, have a conversation with a pretty girl, manage to thank Booker and Sallie properly, and share a laugh with Timbo and Froggie. It was as if I was waiting for the right person to speak with, and that person was somehow waiting for me, to hear my story, to siphon this well of silence. I sensed I must be patient and that there was someone being patient in waiting for me.

PART TWO

Memphis

CHAPTER FIVE

Memphis, Tennessee, 1959

Mayor Edmund Orgill didn't feel well and was slumped in the back of his black sedan en route to a meeting downtown. He was a tall man, handsome and unusually thoughtful in his politics. He exuded the elegance of Southern gentrification but had been successful in getting elected because of his unexpected humbleness. He looked out of the window at his police escort. "I wish they wouldn't do that; it makes me feel ridiculous," he said.

The driver in the front seat looked back. "You all right, sir? You haven't said a word up to now...wish they wouldn't do what, sir?"

"Follow me around with those damned flashing lights and sirens, that's what," replied the mayor.

He never liked the attention, and here he was in 1959, running again for a job he had resisted the first time. Civic leaders had convinced him he had a responsibility to the community for the fortune his family had accumulated over three generations wholesale hardware. The job had not come without personal and financial sacrifice, and this morning he felt particularly weary.

"You're not my regular driver. Who are you?" the mayor asked.

"Your regular man has the stomach virus. My name is Moses, sir. Don't you worry; I've been drivin' for this company for over twenty-five years. I know my way around. I used to be Boss Crump's driver, sure did."

Orgill perked up. "Crump's driver? Moses, did you say? I'll bet you've got some interesting tales to tell about those rides."

For almost half a century, Edward Hull "Boss" Crump had ruled local and state politics; he was iron-fisted, yet alluring in his charm. He was outrageous in appearance, with a carnival barker's beguilement. His shock of white hair was offset by bushy, dark, caterpillar eyebrows that could not be hidden by his disproportionately circular eyeglasses. The "Crump machine" had a reputation as one of the most powerful and arrogant political dynasties in the nation. In countless ways, Memphis had prospered under his vigilance, but Crump's approach to democracy was controversial.

Moses made a left turn onto Union Avenue and headed for the Rotary meeting at the Peabody, where the mayor was scheduled to speak. "Yes, sir, he was somethin', all right. He was gonna get his way, so you best just left him have it, 'cause his henchmen were pretty rough. Do you mind if I say somethin', sir? I may not ever get this chance again."

Orgill looked out at the azaleas and dogwoods exploding in their spring display. "Certainly, I'm your mayor, whether you voted for me or not. You can tell me anything you want."

"Well, now, sir, that's just it. Boss Crump said that, but he didn't mean it. He used us black folks somethin' awful. You know he made a lot of promises to us when election time rolled around, but nuthin' ever changed much." Moses was emboldened when the mayor nodded in agreement. "Back when that Freedom Train was supposed to come to Memphis? Well, it was goin' across the country to show the people the Constitution, that Declaration of Independence, and the Rights Bill. My boys were so excited 'cause they been learnin' about that in school. But Boss Crump said white and black people couldn't mix, so that train didn't come to Memphis. That's just one of the things he did that got to me; there were plenty others."

The Freedom Train incident had been reported in the *New York Times*, and many whites were embarrassed by the coverage. Orgill's unexpected victory over the Crump machine in 1956 was a heady time for Memphis liberals, who envisioned the city moving past its provincial reputation. Orgill listened to the growing civil-rights chorus in the country and was determined to conduct Memphis into the refrain.

In 1957 Little Rock's Central High School in neighboring Arkansas had become the epicenter of the civil-rights movement when nine black students attempted entry into the school. A mob of outraged whites frothed as the police escorted these students into their classes. Outside, as violence erupted, fear for the black students' safety resulted in their being removed from the school. The incident became national news when a showdown between Arkansas governor Orval Faubus and President Eisenhower culminated in the president's activation of the US Army's 101st Airborne Division to take control of the students' entry into classes. The ten-thousand-man Arkansas National Guard was federalized, which removed control from the governor. Faubus had directly challenged the federal government's authority and tested the US Supreme Court's landmark 1954 decision in *Brown v. Board of Education*.

Across the Mississippi River, Memphians were mesmerized. Whites began to see integration as a threat, while to blacks it became a possibility. Quietly and without incident, Orgill began to integrate public facilities. He hoped Memphis could learn from the Little Rock crisis and could unify the races for a better community.

"I didn't understand that either, Moses. It's one reason I ran for mayor. I really am trying to make things better, but you know, change comes in small steps. I'm working with the business community to open things up for all our citizens, the parks, the swimming pools, the public facilities. I hope I have your vote, Moses, but I'm not going to lie to you: there is no quick fix for civil rights."

"I know that, sir, but what I wanted to tell you is my people and I know you're tryin'," said Moses. "You know you're the first mayor in decades to beat the Crump machine; that's somethin' in itself, sir. I've got grandchildren now; maybe it'll be better for them."

"It wears me down sometimes," said Orgill. "I tried to put a black man on the board of John Gaston Hospital, and he was very qualified. The next thing I knew was my daughter woke me in the middle of the night screaming someone had set a cross on fire in our front yard. She's just a little girl."

"I heard about that, sir, and I'm sorry it happened," Moses said as he pulled into the Peabody motor court.

Moses parked the car and looked into the back seat at Orgill. "Mr. Mayor, you got my vote and my wife's too. I wanna wish you luck. I'm countin' on you, sir."

The mayor entered the hotel as the famous Peabody ducks were being settled into the lobby fountain, where they would swim until late afternoon. The tradition had started in the 1930s, when the hotel manager and his buddies returned home from a hunting trip and placed live ducks in the fountain. The guests were so enthralled with the sight that the hotel lobby became the home for four mallard hens and a drake that swam there daily until 5:00 p.m., when they were escorted by their duckmaster—to the sounds of the "King Cotton March" by John Philip Sousa—through the lobby, up the elevator, and into their luxury accommodations on the roof.

Orgill usually spoke to a few of the hundreds of visitors who lined up along the ducks' red carpet to watch the ceremony, but today he plodded past the crowd, the enormous flower displays, the marble floors, and sumptuous furnishings. He trudged up the grand staircase one step at a time, with the face of a weary man about to face a jury.

The second-floor ballroom was arrayed in wide, sculpted, gold trim and lighted by enormous European-crystal chandeliers. A childhood friend of Orgill was making the announcements for Rotary events; he acknowledged the mayor as he slipped in the back door, and the applause for the politician, from over three hundred men, was warm.

His friend intended to speak with Orgill. He wanted to tell him he had gone off the rails with this integration

43

thing, and he needed to remember the people who had put him in office.

Edmund greeted his old friend with a weak handshake and all the enthusiasm he could muster, just as a tall gray-haired waiter passed them and tripped on an ill-placed extension cord. Everyone in the room was startled by the crashing sound of a whole tray of dishes sliding into broken pieces.

"Oh, sir, now I'm really in trouble. I never tripped before—and now in front of the mayor. I won't ever live this down," the embarrassed waiter said, as Orgill knelt down to help him. "I'm so sorry, sir."

"We all have bad days; I'm having one myself," Orgill said as he helped to place the shattered cups on the tray. "How long have you worked here?"

"Thirty-six years, sir. I came straight from the farm to the Peabody. I love it here. I've met people from all over the world."

"You just forget this ever happened," Orgill said and pointed in the direction of the extension cord. "I'll have my office call your boss and tell him that cord was in the wrong place. It wasn't your fault. What's your name?"

"James, sir. Jim Bartlett." The waiter watched as Orgill's assistant wrote it down on a small notepad.

The mayor turned to speak to his childhood friend, but when the man reached for a handshake, Orgill grabbed onto his hand for steadiness. His grip was tight, but the look in his eyes was confused, and suddenly his knees buckled with weakness. Orgill's fall to the floor was followed by a collective gasp in the ballroom. The waiter ran to the telephone in the hallway to summon help. Orgill had suffered a stroke. It was not fatal, but he would have to bow out of the mayor's race.

When Moses returned to pick up the mayor at the appointed time and saw the ambulance taking Orgill away, he left with a heavy heart. It was much worse than the driver could have known. The peaceful path of civil-rights reform Memphis had been ambling down would be ambushed by the midnight marauder that was Edmund Orgill's stroke.

CHAPTER SIX

Orgill left the race in 1959, just as the tumultuous 1960s swept in monumental changes for the country, particularly for the South. Freedom Riders and lunch-counter-sit-in protestors tested segregation laws, with mobs, riots, and beatings leading the evening-news stories televised into the nation's living rooms. In 1962 the first black student was admitted to the University of Mississippi, assisted by five hundred members of the US marshals, army troops, and the National Guard.

In the inflammatory year of 1963, civil-rights activist Medgar Evers was murdered in Jackson, Mississippi; police dogs were unleashed in Birmingham, Alabama, on protestors in what became known as the Bull Connor incident; and four little girls were killed in a church bombing. That same year 250,000 people in Washington listened as Dr. Martin Luther King delivered his "I Have a Dream" speech, and

President John F. Kennedy was assassinated. Protests and violence over civil rights dominated the decade's headlines.

From the diverse group of candidates left in the mayor's race when Orgill dropped out, a former Crump lieutenant, Henry Loeb III, emerged as the winner and was sworn in for the first time in 1960. Late in his term, he resigned to settle business problems within his family's large holdings of laundries and other investments. He was reelected in 1968 with what he felt was a clean slate for his personal and business life.

The Memphis of 1968 was a city famous for its beauty and downtown stores that were the bustling retail center for three states. The growing, vibrant medical community was progressive, and there was particular pride in St. Jude Children's Hospital, founded by entertainer Danny Thomas to research childhood cancers.

Through all the turmoil, Memphis remained a well-mannered town with traditional principles based on home, family, and faith. Though geographically centered in the middle of the racial unrest, Memphis largely missed the worst of it. Yet threatening headlines about antiwar protests; rebellious, drugged-up teenagers; and violent civil-rights actions from distant cities made citizens uneasy.

As Loeb prepared to enter office, civil rights were not much on his mind. He felt the city's minorities should be grateful for the progress made since Orgill had begun the slow progression toward integration. They weren't. To black leaders, Loeb's second term represented a regression into the days of Boss Crump and marginalization of their political aspirations.

It was in this political climate of black disappointment and white apprehension that on February 1, 1968, a housewife in a quiet, leafy east Memphis neighborhood read a story in the morning's newspaper that caught her attention. She reached for the telephone in her spacious kitchen, with its large street-view window. It was a low-slung, long ranch house of light brick with a new swimming pool in the backyard.

She called her best friend. "Doris, I just saw in the paper that Elvis and Priscilla's baby is due any minute. Do you think it's a boy or a girl?" she giggled into the phone. "If it's a girl, I hope she doesn't make her wear a little beehive hairdo and black eyeliner like she does."

It was cold and rainy, a good day for gossiping with a friend, and the housewife watched through the window as a garbage truck stopped in front of her home. When she heard shouts from the street, her tone changed to seriousness. "Doris, hold on, something's happening outside. I'll be right back."

The scene unfolding outside the woman's home was horrific. The driver had jumped out of the garbage truck into the cold and rain when he heard a commotion from the back of the vehicle. An electric malfunction had caused the plate that compacted the trash to begin grinding on its own. The driver raced to the cab and pushed the safety switch over and over and over, but the compressor continued to smash.

It was only then that the driver realized that his two co-workers had moved to the back of the truck to escape the weather and were desperately trying to escape the mashing, mashing, mashing of the compactor. Their screams were terrible as the men's bones snapped and crunched from the smashing metal flattening their bodies into the garbage.

The traumatized, crying housewife who witnessed it all told reporters, "The driver was standing there at the end of the truck, and the machine was moving. He tried to stop it," she said. "Their bodies went in headfirst, and their legs were hanging out. It looked like the truck just swallowed them whole."

The next day, the newspaper reported with glowing, front-page headlines that the King of Rock and Roll had become a father. The baby was named Lisa Marie Presley, and Elvis was already infatuated with her. Buried deep inside the *Commercial Appeal* was a small piece that noted two Memphis garbagemen had been crushed to death in a tragic accident. There was no reference to the men's families or their backgrounds. The birth of Lisa Marie and the deaths of the garbagemen had occurred within an hour of one another, but few would have guessed which event would have the most lasting influence.

Elvis and those unfortunate men had more in common than the casual observer could have known. Elvis had grown up in black neighborhoods. His father went to jail and provided little support for the family, while his mother often depended on government assistance and subsidized housing to survive. He roamed the Beale Street district congregating with the black horn players and singers. He daydreamed about wearing flashy clothes like those showcased in the Lansky Brothers' shop window.

He overcame stage fright, grew his trademark sideburns, and slicked his hair back with rose oil in Memphis, and it was at the Overton Park Shell that his unique hip gyrations, caused by his bundled nerves, would first arouse the hormones of proper teenage girls and make them screaming, crying fanatics. His pulsing rhythms made a perfect alloy of the black and white cultures that would send parents over the edge and teenagers to the record stores.

The black garbagemen who worked the alleyways and backyards of Memphis were paid $1.80 an hour—and not paid at all when the inclement-weather policy was enforced. Their white counterparts had a higher salary, inclement-weather pay, and better benefits. Though it was not a legal necessity, Mayor Loeb insisted their surviving families be given $500 for burial expenses and one month's additional salary. The mayor felt he had met the moral obligation of the city, and that would be the end of this sad story.

Loeb was mistaken. By the end of 1968, Elvis, the city, and the garbagemen would enter a world stage none could have imagined. Appearing on network television in what would became known as the pivotal "'68 comeback special," Elvis reinvented himself and resumed his career with record-breaking, sold-out performances and chart-topping hits.

For the garbagemen, that cold February day of shouldering, stinking refuse running down their backs into their shoes was so defeating that no individual could muster the residual strength to mount much of a protest over the deaths and their work conditions. But their collective stamina for a fight surprised themselves and the nation. The brutal death of two of their own had unleashed decades of directionless rage into a focused fury. Memphis and these men were about to become the leading players in what was sometimes the inspiring pageant and sometimes the ridiculous circus that was civil rights in America.

CHAPTER SEVEN

"Who the hell do those men think they are?" Loeb railed in his office after receiving notice the garbage workers had a list of demands. "I'll be damned if this is going to get us off course. I've only been in office two months. Just because two idiots didn't have enough sense to stay out of the back of a compression truck, we aren't going off budget over *this*."

The accident had given disgruntled workers a platform to raise other troubling issues that before had seemed unlikely to make an impression on municipal officials. Union reps informed the city that the garbagemen were concerned about raises, overtime, and slowing truck routes, and they wanted a safety program. Also written on that document was one more item, the fissure, which would ultimately erupt into the streets of Memphis: payroll deductions for union dues, which would mean recognition of the union by the city.

"I'm not recognizing the union. You said it was illegal; that's our story, and we're stickin' with it," Loeb screamed into the phone at the city's attorney. "I won this election on a fiscal-responsibility platform, and I'm not going to be lynched over this. Got it? Don't argue with me." Loeb slammed down the phone.

"No one owns a piece of me." It was a favorite line of Henry Loeb's, and it was true. Loeb was a man of contradictions. He was an imposing individual at six foot five inches, and he was capable of using his size to bully—as he surely must have as commander of a PT boat in World War II. However, in his political campaigns, he was convivial and warm. He was handsome, with a deep left part in his dark, thinning hair. His smile was broad, but his expression could darken suddenly when he was displeased, his lips becoming a thin line, his hands tightening into fists.

He purposely feigned a Southern simpleton persona—one that disguised an aristocratic education from Phillips at Andover and Brown University. He married the 1950 Cotton Carnival Queen and spoke in racist tones with his elite friends at social gatherings, yet he ran his family's chain of laundries with a mostly black staff. Even his faith was not without contradiction. He would turn his back on his Jewish heritage and become an Episcopalian to please his wife. One characteristic about Loeb had no contradictions: he was a stubborn man.

When the local-union stewards walked into the mayor's office for the first time to discuss trash collection and the accident, he spoke in a calm, patriarchal manner: "Now, gentlemen, this union is selling your people a bill of goods.

The city of Memphis is not going to bow down. You and I both know we have no liability in this tragedy.

"Most of your men are uneducated, and that makes them easy prey for the promises of these Yankee union people," Loeb continued. "We'll be glad to consider some of this when we begin talks for the city's budget next year, but the money is just not there right now."

Hundreds of hopeful workers packed into Clayborn Temple all afternoon to learn the city's response. They played cards, drank coffee together, and were optimistic about their position until the glum-faced union steward returned and announced to the crowd, "This ain't goin' to be easy for you members to swallow," as he recounted the meeting with the mayor.

A speaker sent by the union's national headquarters tried to rouse the men with encouraging messages: "You have an obligation to these men; their families are counting on you to make their deaths mean something. This is our time, and the city cannot ignore you any longer."

The garbagemen were crestfallen over the news and began leaving a few at a time, grumbling as they made their way to the door. From the back of the room, a man who had been silent all morning raised a hand. He was a small, ragged man in his sixties, strengthened by the appalling loss of two of his closest friends; a man who had toted garbage in Memphis for twenty-six years; a man whose wife insisted he leave his stinking clothes outside the door each day so her home would not be overcome with the stench; a man who had had enough; a man who rose and shouted in a commanding voice that belied his stature, "Let's fight."

The room of several hundred arguing men went silent for an extended time. Someone shouted, "Let's have a vote," and when the ballots were counted, it was nearly unanimous; the garbagemen would strike.

"*Strike!*" Henry Loeb screamed at the city's attorney. "They wanna strike; well, that is just fine. Garbage is gonna be picked up. You can bet on it!" Loeb was now standing over the attorney and pointing his finger. "Not one of these men is going to have a job with this city if they don't call this thing off right now. I'm gonna break that union's back for good."

From the point of view of union executives in New York City, the plan to strike was ill-conceived. February was not the time for a garbage strike; better to wait for July, when the stinking refuse made more of an impression and Memphis had a ready labor pool of unemployed workers who could replace the garbagemen. Many of their Memphis members were older, and the union's concern was they were not financially or physically ready to sustain a prolonged strike. But they were in it now, and the union's national office had no choice but to back the trash collectors.

When the balding P. J. Ciampa, with his dark-circled, hooded eyes, arrived from New York City, he was escorted with other union executives into Loeb's office with expectations the matter could come to a quick resolve.

Loeb perched behind his large desk at one end of the dark-paneled room, with the city's crest cast in a huge medallion hanging on the wall behind him. Dozens of framed historical scenes hung on the walls, many of them photographic depictions of cotton being hauled into the city for the spot market. The desk was elevated on an eight-inch platform, which, combined with Loeb's height, made him appear over seven feet tall. Low couches and chairs lighted only by fluorescent fixtures forced visitors to look up and squint at the mayor.

"Well, hello, Mister Chiampy. I heard a lot about ya," Loeb drawled. "Glad to see ya. Welcome to Memphis. Now let's talk."

After the Northerners regained their composure from Loeb's deliberate mispronunciation of Ciampa's name, they sensed an early edge in their talks when Loeb admitted to being a novice at labor negotiations. The union men were street-smart and smug, but they misjudged Henry Loeb. He was everything these men were not. He was beautifully educated, wealthy, and the son of a prominent family. He was also willful and wily.

"I been thinkin' a lot 'bout all this, and I think the fairest way to handle these negotiations is with a camera and reporters in the room, just to keep all of us honest. Y' know what I mean, fellas?" Loeb said.

"Cameras?" the startled Ciampa replied. "How in God's name are we going to negotiate in public? No, Mayor Loeb, we'll call in the reporters when we've reached an agreement. This shouldn't be too difficult."

"Now, Mr. Chiampy, my citizens have a right to know what's goin' on here," said Loeb. "These meetings are going to be open. This is the city's business, and you might as well make up your mind to like it or go back to New York."

Loeb had a talent for the dramatic, and he intended to use his entire arsenal on these men, whom he saw as interlopers. Memphis television viewers were treated to a spectacle of wills between two men: one played the part of placating local sheriff, and the other was cast as a greasy, used-car salesman.

On one early TV broadcast, Loeb drawled, "Now, Mister Chiampy, you may have been able to convince Mayor John Lindsay to open his city's pocketbook over a garbage strike, but I don't care what Lindsay did. You're talkin' to a country boy. This is not New York." Loeb raised his hand, pointed his finger upward, and looked straight into the camera. "I live here, and my kids live here, and I am not going to play around with the health of this city."

Back across the Mississippi River in Arkansas, Booker Benton watched the news from Memphis during his dinner hour in the evenings, with Dewdrop at his feet. "Sallie, this might get interestin'. I don't think this strike is gonna be over for a while. Mayor Loeb and this Eye-talian don't like each other very much."

Ciampa was visibly unnerved in daily meetings when the television lights flashed on and the camera whirred to life. He returned to his hotel room every evening in a cold sweat, wondering what clip the news programs would pull from the day to make him look like a gangster.

"Keep your big mouth shut!" Ciampa once blasted across the Memphis airways, shown poking his finger at Loeb's nose.

On the morning drive from his hotel to the meeting site, he saw an increasing number of black-and-orange stickers on car bumpers, telephone poles, and store windows that read CIAMPA GO HOME.

The two local newspapers gave editorial support to the mayor and urged the garbagemen to go back to work. Loeb reported he was strengthened in resolve by the dozens of letters of support he professed to be receiving every day.

Heels on both sides dug in, Loeb began one meeting with: "Now, sir, the mayor can't be in the position of bargaining with anyone who is breaking the law, and the Tennessee high court has ruled this strike illegal."

"What crime have these men committed?" Ciampa implored. "They say they don't want to pick up stinking garbage for starvation wages. Is that a crime?"

"The fact is you are breaking the law." Loeb stood his ground.

"Put your halo in your pocket, quit the country-boy routine, and let's get realistic," retorted Ciampa.

Loeb shot back with, "Chiampy, you're a son of a bitch."

So it went broadcast after broadcast, as TV viewers soon forgot the critical issues of the strike and looked forward to the nightly reports of the two men, who lined up like cocks in a fight each day.

At Clayborn Temple, determined garbagemen refused to be forgotten, and it wasn't long before the numbers of marching men in the downtown streets became a substantial swell. Within the first weeks, someone printed placards that read "I AM A MAN." The author of that slogan knew that words have power. Demonstrating with those signs, these former apparitions of Memphis alleyways and backyards, who had toted on their heads tubs of rotting refuse, straightened their ragged clothes, lifted their chins, and commanded their physical forms to come forth. For the first time, they were going to be seen.

Mayor Loeb was winning the local battle, which was what he cared about. "Look, the newspapers are supporting us. We were elected on a promise to these citizens we would be fiscally responsible, and that's what we're gonna do," he said in a meeting with his deputies. "The city council wants us to settle, but it's just not going to happen."

"I feel terrible for these men; they've lost two of their own. I know what that feels like; I lost friends in the war. But these poor men," Loeb continued, "they are just not smart enough to see the union is exploiting them. They don't care about the garbagemen; they're just trying to promote their own agenda. Not in my town, they won't."

It wasn't long before the strike got ugly. When the thin veneer of polite behavior was stripped away by the strike, a disturbing truth emerged. Memphis was a city plagued by fear, anger, resentment, and hatred on both sides of the racial divide. City councilmen, civic leaders, and ministers—both black and white—received death threats, obscene phone calls, and cruel letters. No one had to announce any allegiances publicly; loyalty was displayed by the positioning of their garbage. Those who supported the mayor brought their trash to the street for the first time in their lives, so the newly hired trash collectors could retrieve it. In the yards of those who supported the strike, garbage was left to rot in stinking, putrid mounds.

There was a macing and beating incident on Main Street, followed by harsh finger-pointing from the city and the union and rally cries from the black community for more forceful tactics to get Loeb's attention where necessary.

Somewhere in the turmoil of the mayor battling city-council members and his daily effort to get a skeleton crew of collectors, together with citizens trying for the first time to remember to push their garbage cans to the street, a subtle switch in perceptions occurred. From the pulpit of black churches came protests that this was not just a labor dispute but was a civil-rights cause. Tempers and patience were being tested on both sides. Black leaders began to take stock of their strength and work on ways to keep the momentum from waning. One of the group had a long and trusted relationship with Dr. Martin Luther King.

"I'll give Martin a call tomorrow to see if he can be of assistance to our cause," he said.

CHAPTER EIGHT

"Martin Luther King! For God's sake, why have they called him?" Loeb shouted at the city attorney. "I wish Boss Crump was still with us; he would have chased these bastards out of town long ago."

The attorney leaned over the conference table with his head in his hand and listened to Loeb bellow on about the strike. "Henry, maybe it's time we looked into some alternatives. Crump would have been the first to tell you that you have to give a little to get a little. Why don't we offer to phase in a wage increase over three years and give them what they want, except for the union recognition? I think that might go a long way toward getting this thing settled."

Loeb pounded on the table with his fist and snarled back, "You either get on board with me or you get off. Now get out of here, and don't come back until you have decided whose side you're on. Martin Luther King doesn't scare me one damn bit."

To supporters, detractors, and everyone in between, the Atlanta preacher Martin Luther King Jr. symbolized American civil rights. The thunderous 1960s swept social, economic, political, behavioral, and historical norms into a swirling storm, tossed them around, and then abandoned them into an unrecognizable muddle, and from that chaos, King emerged as a reluctant icon. He loaned his eloquence, poise, and credibility to the Montgomery, Alabama, bus boycott in 1955 and then was pressed into service to be the face of the movement. He could not have imagined then that history had prepared for him a potholed path of hatred, death threats, arrests, physical harm, and the near loss of his family. For a young man who had just turned thirty-nine, he wore a mask of exceptional world-weariness.

When the telephone call came to King about the garbage strike, he was in a fragile state of mind. His minions noted his preoccupation with morbid thoughts about his own mortality. He was overweight, drinking more than he should, sleeping little, and keeping the company of women outside his marriage. Here was a man revered for his commitment to nonviolence and idolized for his strength and courage, yet he was slipping badly in the court of public opinion. He was beginning to look like a relic in his own movement.

Though President Lyndon Johnson and the Reverend King together had a storied record on civil- and voting-rights legislation, the president had recently called King "that nigger preacher" because of his opposition to the Vietnam War. Urban blacks were becoming restless with the plodding progress of the nonviolent movement and were using civil disorder to push for a more forceful message.

Most of King's associates within the Southern Christian Leadership Conference felt his enthusiastic plans to mount a historic march of poor people into Washington in the late spring of 1968 was ill advised, a symptom of his sleepless nights and a somewhat pathetic attempt to restore his public face. They berated him often for taking on too many local issues, so, while they listened as King spoke to Memphis on the telephone and agreed to come march with the garbagemen, many in the room rolled their eyes.

But King was far ahead of his advisers. He was driven by a force greater than himself, a force that ignored his exhaustion, demanded his attention like a sore foot, and shoved his personal and family needs away. He fed the force with his life and prayed that if he obeyed, there would be a day he could regain control, return home from the road, and relish his accomplishments. Now the force insisted that poor people of all races—people whose wages were not enough to even modestly provide for their families, people who were left in the wake of America's soaring success—should have a champion. He would march these lowly spirits into the nation's capital and encamp them in the city by the hundred thousands, and they would be heard. King felt America had made a legislative down payment on civil rights but had yet to open its coffers for opportunity truly equal for all.

Whispering in his ear, the force told King there was no better example of the working poor than these garbagemen, many of whom had come to the city from the Mississippi Delta cotton fields, thinking Memphis would provide them with a better life. If his presence catapulted their story onto the front pages of national newspapers, then it was a winning hand for everybody. Plans were finalized: he would arrive in Memphis on March 18 and speak at Mason Temple that evening.

King arrived in Memphis with just barely enough time to reach the immense Pentecostal Mason Temple at the appointed hour. When he slipped into the side door, he paused for a moment of prayer and felt gratitude for this rare moment of peace in his life.

He had been promised a capacity crowd. But, in fact, there were more than fifteen thousand searching souls, standing in the aisles, sitting on the steps, and pouring out of the doorways. A pathway had to be cleared for King to enter the hall as thunderous applause followed him to the podium. He had a catch in his throat and fought back tears. The past few years had been tough. He knew he was losing relevance, and his lifelong commitment to nonviolence was in question. He knew that support for the People's March on Washington was not widespread even among his own counsel.

But here in this place were people who were willing and hopeful that his message would be manna in the desert for their cause. Thirty-six days of government hampering and stonewalling had led the garbagemen and their supporters to this place. And this place, where the frustrations of Martin Luther King and these lowly sanitation workers came to dance with destiny, was charged in anticipation. As King looked over the crowd, he thought—this place, these people—it was all perfect. It was the perfect way to launch his Poor People's Campaign, and his weariness rescinded.

King started slowly with greetings and acknowledgments, and then, with a deliberate voice, he said, "You are demonstrating that we are tied in a single garment of destiny, and that if one black person suffers, if one black person is down, we are all down."

He noted that all labor has significance and that the value of the garbage collector is no lower than that of the physician.

Shouts from the crowd spurred King to implore America to use her vast wealth to end poverty. With his gift for poetic language he described buildings so tall they kissed the sky, bridges that spanned the seas, space ships and airplanes so powerful they "are able to dwarf distance and place time in chains." Even with all those resources he claimed to hear the "God of the universe saying, I was hungry and fed me not. I was naked and ye clothed me not."

He continued with a call for the economic equality and noted those brave enough to position themselves at white-only lunch counters were wasting their efforts if they were unable to afford a meal.

To the strikers he spoke about their struggles of being out of work for many days and encouraged them not to despair; he told them that anything worthwhile requires sacrifice. Calling for stronger action, he urged that a general work stoppage of domestic and blue collar laborers might be necessary.

He asked of them to make this the beginning of the Washington movement and ended with: "We will build a new Memphis and bring about the day when every valley shall be exalted, every mountain and hill will be made low. The rough places will be made plain, and the crooked places straight, and the glory of the Lord shall be revealed, and all flesh shall see it together. We will be able to build right here a city which has foundations."

Many in the audience were weeping; others were on their feet shouting with joy. Their crusade had been confirmed by the one person who best represented the plight of the working man in America. People everywhere would hear that Dr. Martin Luther King had taken up their cause.

Behind the scenes, strike leaders conferred with King's people, imploring them to agree for their leader to return to Memphis for a march, which would have national news coverage.

Flush from the adoration of the crowd, King quickly accepted. The mood was jubilant. The date was set for the coming Friday, March 22.

CHAPTER NINE

S pring is beautiful in Memphis, Tennessee. Early bloomers like hellebores, daffodils, and crocuses can sometimes be seen by the last week in February. Rain from thunderstorms rolling across the Mississippi River, followed by sunny days, bring azaleas and dogwood trees back to life. The temperature can make dramatic shifts until mid-May, but that doesn't stop eager baseball players and golfers from throwing on jackets and getting outside.

The morning of March 21 began drearily, with low clouds and spitting rain. There was a cold snap, which was annoying but not really unusual. But when the rain had turned to snow by noon, there was mild surprise expressed in a city whose annual snowfall amounts are less than six inches. When the flakes became, as someone described them, "as large as dollar pancakes," things started to get interesting. By the morning of March 22, when King was scheduled to arrive, there was over sixteen inches of snow on the ground; city traffic and commerce came to a halt under the second-largest snowfall in the city's history.

When King received notice that the march had been delayed until the following Thursday, March 28, he went about his day in Atlanta thinking little of the postponement. But back in Memphis, a few of the strike leaders had an uneasy feeling, prompting one of them to say, "Well, the Lord has done it again: it's a white world."

On the morning of the rescheduled march, as King left the New York City area, nothing could squelch his good mood. This would be the last event before he headed to Washington for the Poor People's Campaign.

Back in Memphis on a brilliant, cloudless morning, the garbagemen and their families were beaming with excitement. They were joined by supporters from all over the Mid-South, among them prominent clergy and politicians. Tucked inside that crowd of senior citizens, babies in strollers, and elementary-school kids with their mothers were petty criminals, drunken fools, and a large number of unruly high-school boys taking advantage of an excuse to cut class.

Wilber Miller, a white, longtime Memphis police officer who had gained the trust of black citizens through the years with his countless hours of patrolling in their neighborhoods, stood on Beale Street near the middle of the procession. Lately Miller's back ached more than usual from a war injury he had sustained while parachuting from airplanes into enemy territories in the pitch dark.

Twenty years in the service, along with time served in France during the war and his police background, afforded Miller a keener sense for impending trouble than the ordinary cop. He said a silent prayer: "Lord, please let me get home in time for dinner; we're having fried chicken, and I've been thinking about it all day."

Miller spotted several young men from his beat who were speaking loudly and laughing; he walked over to them. "You boys need to settle down. This march isn't playtime. Let's just get through this, and everybody's gonna get home safe."

One youth ripped the placard he was carrying with a hateful, vulgar message from its three-foot stick and brandished it like a sword. Other boys quickly joined in the sword game. "Boys, come on now," said Miller, "let's put the sticks away. Don't you know who is coming here today? Why, Martin Luther King, he wouldn't want you to act like that."

"Screw you, honky pig," came the response from the crowd, followed by loud laughter among the boys.

Miller took the shoulder of a young man. "Son, I've known you since you were born. I held you in my arms when you were a baby. Your daddy is a fine, hardworking man. I need you to help me settle your friends down."

The boy jerked his shoulder away from Miller, stared back at the police officer, and then spit at him. Officers had been ordered to pull back from the marchers to minimize friction, so Miller backed away.

Impatient marchers, agitated by King's late arrival, grew more restless as a false rumor that a student had been killed by police circulated through the crowd. Communication from the front to the back of the line was nonexistent.

When King finally arrived in a white Lincoln Continental, exhilaration rippled through the crowd. The civil-rights hero linked arms with marchers, and the massive line, which filled the width of the street and stretched for several city blocks, lunged forward in hope.

Within minutes, sounds of shattering glass and shouting infused the atmosphere. Police Officer Miller was frantic as he watched the young man he had spoken with and his friends smash the windows along Beale Street and loot the stores. He heard one of them scream, "Burn it down, baby!" as a can of gasoline and matches materialized from within the crowd.

Neither King nor the strike leaders could see the chaos, but they could certainly hear it. Panic-stricken, they worked to calm the crowd, but as they tried to move forward, a demarcation line of police in riot gear and gas masks emerged to seal off the road ahead. After only seven blocks and twenty-five minutes, the city of Memphis found itself in a full-scale riot. Before police could regain control, two hundred buildings had been vandalized or burned, and a suspected looter was killed.

"No, I'm not leaving," Dr. King shouted at associates, who were desperately trying to extract him from the crowd. "We've got to get this under control; leave me alone and let me do my work." But his terrified protectors would have none of it. Dr. King was shuttled away to a hotel room overlooking the Mississippi River to watch from a room high above the fires and mayhem.

The event was intended to give the Poor People's Campaign a launch pad. Instead, national-television-news shows reported that Dr. King had stirred up hatred in Memphis and then abandoned his post when the violence broke out. Never mentioned in the paper was the fact that not one garbageman or strike leader was ever arrested.

King spent the rest of the afternoon with the covers over his head, dazed from the events and knowing that his wrecked reputation and the obvious damage to the Poor People's Campaign would mean everything in his life had now changed. His position in history, the movement, and the plans for the Washington event were all in jeopardy.

PART THREE

Across the River and Into the Divide

CHAPTER TEN

The Marianna Tasty Treat was the late-afternoon gathering spot for after-school kids and dusty farm workers alike. My friends and I met there most afternoons to grab a hamburger and then go to the small Chinese-owned grocery store next door for a beer. We sat on the curb with our burgers and beers and plotted our weekends together.

When Froggie's truck drove into the Tasty Treat driveway, it was on two wheels. He hoisted it into park and jumped out with a big grin. "We're goin' to Memphis."

"What do you mean, we're goin' to Memphis?" I asked, never even looking at Froggie, but instead at the menu board over the jukebox.

"That black preacher from Atlanta showed up this morning, and now the place is in flames. They've called up the National Guard; we're leavin' in an hour."

Froggie and Timbo used the pay phone outside the store to call home. We broke speed limits as we raced to the armory, where men scrambled to get their gear loaded on the bus with guns and tear gas secured in trucks that would precede us. Froggie was right: within an hour we were seated on the bus and speeding down the highway to Memphis, just as twilight set.

"Can ya believe this? We're gonna get to march down Beale Street and with our guns out. This is gonna be a blast," said Timbo.

"We might get our pictures in the paper. Do you think we could ride in a tank?" Froggie asked.

I shrugged. "Maybe. That might be fun." It was hard for me to share their enthusiasm because once I put on my military fatigues, I was reminded of my brother, who would have thought us inane and childish for wanting to play war.

"It's not like we're headed to 'Nam," I said. Timbo and Froggie refused to be brought down by my dark mood and got together for a poker game.

Our convoy of surrounding guard units was five miles long when we crossed the Mississippi River bridge in the darkness, with the Rivermont Hotel in sight. Dr. King was still there, counting his losses after the morning melee. I didn't know much about Dr. King, but I remembered hearing the older men at the farm complain about how he was going around the country stirring up trouble. My feelings about him were ambivalent.

"Do either of you know how all this got started? What set off the riots?" I asked.

"Who cares," said Froggie. "This is gonna be fun." He and Timbo turned their attention back to the poker game.

I knew there had been a garbage strike and that there was tension building between the white and black residents, but I lived in a universe where blacks and whites stayed among their own, and everyone understood their role. I could not imagine things changing much for the black families in my neighborhood.

I had no fear of change. It was a savage who had come into our home and taken my mother as its hostage. I knew that you could go on a simple fishing trip and lose a brother and make a simple bowl of soup and lose a father. But I wasn't clever enough to have an internal barometer for change. Still, change was grinding its way across America, and the inevitable friction was heating to white hot in the city of Memphis, Tennessee.

While Froggie and Timbo played poker, I looked out the bus window as the flat delta unfolded with men still in the fields, working the land even as dark descended. In this rare contemplative mood, I thought about how, even in these fields, a revolution was occurring. The harvest was becoming mechanized, with fancy, expensive equipment that performed with an efficiency measured in scant hours, not days, to cover a field.

The black families I knew growing up were still in their homes next to my neighborhood, but their children were leaving in droves. Many headed for Detroit, Michigan, to work in the booming auto factories, which fed the American appetite to cross our new interstate highways and move away from inner cities to leafy suburbs.

From a radio that someone was playing in the bus came the voice of Walter Cronkite, and it halted all laughter and chatter. A CBS reporter described the scene in Memphis and referenced comments Cronkite had made earlier in the week. His words were a damning editorial on America's military plan in Vietnam and its commanders. Cronkite said, "It is increasingly clear to this reporter that the only rational way out then will be to negotiate, not as victors but as honorable people who lived up to their pledge to defend democracy and did the best they could."

The reporter revealed that President Lyndon Johnson had admitted to his staff that if he had lost Cronkite, he had lost middle America.

To end the silence in the bus, I asked no one in particular, "Where are we going to sleep?" as we entered the gloomy fairgrounds complex.

The Memphis Fairgrounds was a curious mixture of buildings. On one side of the bus was the amusement park, with blazing lights and two smiling but sinister clown faces painted on the entrance doors. On the other was the football stadium of the local college. In between were long cavernous buildings, some with walls and others only roofed so that cattle, sheep, vegetables, and baked goods could be presented to the county fair judges each September.

We parked at the only illuminated building and unloaded our gear. Local national guardsmen greeted us with serious faces as we were joined by at least three hundred other men from surrounding guard units.

"Wow, look at the tear-gas canisters! I've never seen so much ammo. It's kinda scary," Timbo said as we watched hundreds of tear-gas grenades being hauled to one side of the room in crates and bayonets lining the back wall like matches waiting for a strike.

There was no time to meet our fellow soldiers as a commander on a raised platform shouted out names to assign us to groups. Froggie and Timbo were among the first called and placed under the same leader. I watched as they were led away to a different building, unsuspecting that it would be many months before I would again see them.

Finally, I heard, "Cotton Mathis, you're under Bartlett's command," and I was led away with a group of strangers.

Feet shuffling, our group bided time, waiting to meet our commander. One by one, bloated, aging soldiers snapped forward to salute their assignees. At last, a backlit figure emerged from the building into the bus's shadow. Staff Sgt. Boaz Bartlett perforated the darkness to stand and assess us. He was a man so muscled he could have been menacing. He was over six feet and had a clipped stride and efficient pacing. Moving into the light, I caught two note-worthy characteristics I hadn't noticed until now. He had a mangled, bandaged arm, and Staff Sgt. Boaz Bartlett was a black man.

As the light shed our fate, I was fascinated because I knew no one in my group had ever taken orders from a man of color. The soldier next to me had a different reaction. Hearing a great hawking sound, I jumped out of the way as he spat on the right boot of Sgt. Bartlett.

In a single movement, the black officer bent, scraped up the spit, and raked it down the front of the soldier's surprised face. "Did you drop something?" he asked. All chatter subsided.

The second the sergeant was out of earshot, I heard the same question over and over that night in the lonely, drab hall: "Who the hell is Boaz Bartlett?"

After supper a group of men surrounded one of the cooks, a heavyset man who wore a dirty apron and whose sleeves were rolled up to reveal a series of dragon-figure tattoos. He was a retired-career army cook who had joined the National Guard after his last tour in Vietnam because he missed the action, he was divorced, and he had lost touch with his children during his military career. The cook was a Memphis native and very familiar with our commander's background.

"Boaz Bartlett is a gen-u-ine American hero. Y'know, if it were you and you were in a helicopter crash, you wouldn't rightly care what color the man who pulled you out was, now would ya?" He had us all mesmerized at that point. "Bartlett rescued the pilot and two men from a burnin' helicopter and then killed three of the enemy to boot. He won a Silver Star for that."

"What's he doin' here?" one of our group asked.

"I dunno, I think he mighta hurt his arm, but he did tell me he was anxious to get back to 'Nam. The guard musta asked him to help out for the time bein'. He's a good man. The Memphis newspaper put his picture on the front page; I think they wanted to use him as an example to show we ain't prejudiced or somethin'."

Whether we take our given names and let them become the definition of our lives or the cosmic forces around us know our destiny and name us for their purposes is up for debate. But our name walks with us.

In the Bible's Book of Ruth, Boaz noticed Ruth and her widowed daughter-in-law working in the fields. In a generous, protective gesture, Boaz married Ruth and thereby saved both women from a perilous future. When Boaz and Ruth had a son, the women's family lineage was saved, and that son is mentioned in the New Testament as an ancestor of Jesus. Boaz is a very important, pious figure in the Christian faith.

Another Biblical reference is the Boaz pillar, which was one of the two frontal columns of Solomon's mighty temple. If true, the Boaz pillar would have functioned to support the structure of Israel's king, the son of David, at the height of his powers. Lying in my cot, waiting for sleep, I thought about these stories from my Sunday-school lessons and wondered whether Sgt. Boaz Bartlett truly would measure up to his name.

In the morning, breakfast was soggy oatmeal and over-cooked bacon, served with grumbling over the uncomfortable cots and lack of sleep. I had a restless night, not because of the cot but because I was away from home and my friends, and I felt even more alone than usual.

Bartlett lined us up in front of him. "I need volunteers to patrol neighborhoods," he said. Eight men raised their hands. "The remainder of you will be worked into the marching units who support the tanks that patrol downtown streets."

I took a deep breath and exhaled; a downtown patrol would increase the chances I would be reunited with my friends. We were breaking rank to get about the day's duties when Bartlett said, "One more thing, men: I need one volunteer to partner with me and work the downtown area on foot. It might require that man to stay in Memphis a while after the guard sends the rest of you home."

At my back a firm but invisible hand pushed me forward.

"I'll do it," I said. What if I had known that hand had the power to rechannel the Mississippi River and that the course of my life would become as helpless as an eddy in its mighty portage? Would I have been able to resist the unrelenting push?

CHAPTER ELEVEN

Through the long night of the aborted march, King's associates moved from the window to the television. From above, they watched the burning buildings and unruly throngs throwing bricks and looting stores. On the television, news broadcasters, using serious tones, reported what was happening beneath the expensive suite in the sky, with its new, blue carpet and white, modern furnishings.

Ralph Abernathy was King's most trusted friend and adviser, the man who traveled with him, who shared the most intimate moments of his personal life. "All of you need to settle down and now!" he said, trying to quell the complaining going on in the room. "I know many of you didn't want to come to Memphis, but we're in it now, and the whining's not gonna make it any better."

The grave voice of Chet Huntley cut into the network programming to bring a special report on the riot; it drew the attention away from Abernathy. "Turn off that damn television," Abernathy said. "Can't you see what's goin' on by just looking out the window? Sit down and let's figure out what we're gonna do next." Someone ordered coffee and sandwiches, and the men got to work.

In the adjoining room, King was in bed, paralyzed with grief and fear, and Abernathy was covering for him. He had insisted they come to Memphis. It was supposed to be a brief publicity stop before the Poor People's Campaign in Washington. Now not only was that in jeopardy, but his entire legacy lay in the balance. He vacillated between self-pity and defiance. In the wee hours, he devised a plan: he would return to Memphis and lead a peaceful march for the world to see. That march would have far more news coverage than the original one and would be a recommitment to his agenda of nonviolence.

Even in the morning, when the *Commercial Appeal* called him "Chicken a la King," and other newspapers were even more vitriolic, he was undaunted. He dressed and went into the room where Abernathy and his followers had been working through the night. "I have made a decision; there will be no discussion on this matter," he said. "We'll return to Memphis, and we'll have a peaceful march for all the world to see. Our mission is to prove to one and all that in the Lord's eyes, these garbagemen have value and their claim on equality is sound. Now get busy; I want the details of this worked out when I finish meeting with the Invaders."

The Invaders were young leaders of an inflammatory faction that had publicly denounced King's peaceful methods as ineffective and that many accused of inciting the riot. They were a somber lot when they were led into a meeting with Dr. King. When King entered the room, he was wearing an aqua-green shirt and a shiny suit. One of the group would remember the softness of his hands and said, "When he came into the room, it seemed like all of a sudden there was a real rush of wind, and peace and calm settled over everything. You could feel peace around that man." Expecting a comprehensive and angry assessment of their failures, the young people were much more shaken by Dr. King's soft tone.

"Come over here, gentlemen, and look out the window with me," he said. "You see those smoking buildings and the goods from those stores strewn over the street? Some of those establishments were owned by black families; their livelihood has been destroyed. I point these things out not to berate you but simply to face the results of violence.

"I want you to look at this scene, and I want you to never forget how little has been accomplished for such a high cost. I forgive you for whatever part you may have played in this. Now let's put this behind us and move on."

King led the young men back to a small conference table. "I am coming back to Memphis in April, and we'll sit down and talk. You fellows have been working this area, and you deserve not to be left out. I need you to help me repair the damage, and we must march peacefully through the streets of Memphis. Will you help me?"

One of the leader of the Invaders left the meeting awestruck. "It was one of the few times in my life when I wasn't fighting something. It was as if the events of the previous day had never happened, and I was in a psychotherapy session," he said.

Later King faced a press conference with determined dignity. As one person noted, Memphis was to be either a "dam or a gate" for Dr. King. When his group returned to Atlanta, there would be arguments and dissension in the ranks. But King finally prevailed. They would return to Memphis with plans made to stage a peaceful march.

CHAPTER TWELVE

Sgt. Bartlett looked me up and down. "You sure you want to do this? You might be here a few weeks, but you'll be paid well at the end."

"Yes, sir. Is it okay if I call my employer and tell him I'm staying here?" I asked.

"Sure," he replied. "I'll meet you out front." I called the Chandler farm, told them I was needed in Memphis, and hoped they would hold my job.

I left the building to find Bartlett in the parking lot. He was waiting for me in a dark-blue Chevrolet sedan that was at least ten years old. No matter its age, it was the cleanest car I had ever seen; every inch of the machine was polished.

We left the fairgrounds and drove the midtown streets. "You'll be staying with me at my father's house from now on. There'll be a new commander of our group when they return from assignments tonight. You got any problem staying in a black neighborhood?"

"No, sir, not at all, not if your neighbors don't mind," I answered.

As we entered the downtown area, burned buildings were still smoking, and firemen wetted down whole city blocks to contain any remaining small fires.

Shopkeepers rummaged through trash in the streets, trying to salvage merchandise from their stores and swept broken glass from the sidewalk. The neon sign in front of the popular Arcade Restaurant was broken in half. The older couple who had owned the place for decades surveyed the broken window and burned-out kitchen. In the glass that was left in the window was a sign that read "No Colored Allowed."

Bartlett continued with the details of our assignment: "The guard will say I have been reassigned. You won't be able to return to your unit until this march is over, and Dr. King is out of Memphis. Do you have a problem with that?"

"No, sir," I replied as I looked across the river to Arkansas.

Bartlett's voice tugged me away from my thoughts. "We'll be working the downtown area for the FBI and the Memphis Police Department. We need to wear regular clothes. I'm taking you now to buy a few things, so you can just blend in with the local crowd."

I nodded and looked down a stretch of two blocks where every building was damaged or burned.

"They want a black man and a white man, so we can work our way through the crowds to pick up any suspicious talk. You stay with your people, and I'll stay with mine. We'll go to the Downtown Precinct at the end of the day to report."

I couldn't help myself any longer. "So you're a big hero. Why are doing this? My brother died in Vietnam, and they say you want to go back. Why would anyone want to go back?"

"Don't change the subject; we've got a job to do here, and I'm doing this because the guard asked me to. We'll find a place to meet up a couple of times a day and compare what's going on. Don't discuss this with anyone."

I had gone too far. Bartlett was in no mood for a philosophical discussion.

"I'll be going to the churches and the black neighborhoods to get a feel for what people are saying. You need to walk the streets, get in the crowds, and go to the lunch counters and stores. Just keep your eyes and ears open. We don't want any more riots, and we don't want anyone else to get hurt. You think you can handle this?"

"Yes, sir," I said.

"I don't care about your politics. Your job is to prevent loss of life and property. When Dr. King is safe in Washington, then you can have an opinion. You get out here at the next street and go into that store straight ahead."

Bartlett pointed to a men's store that had managed to escape the riot. "Give the bald man this note. He will help you get the things you need. Don't worry about the bill. I'm going to drive around a while, and I'll meet you back here. Black people aren't allowed in the store."

I did what I was told and stood waiting for Bartlett on the street with my new clothes wrapped in heavy brown paper and tied with string. I wondered how he could be so matter-of-fact about telling me black people were not welcome where I had just been.

As we drove through downtown, he pointed out landmarks and specific areas he wanted me to cover. What few people were on the sidewalks had gathered to watch the armored personnel carriers that were rumbling through the streets.

Two women, who were sweeping the broken window glass in front of Schwab's Department Store, held their hands to their mouths in disbelief as the tanks rolled by. I looked for Froggie and Timbo among the tank escorts who marched in rhythm, with their bayonets high in the air, but I saw no one I recognized.

"Let's go meet my dad. He's got dinner made for us." I nodded, and Boaz added, "We'll get to bed early; we've got to meet with the FBI at six in the morning."

Bartlett's father lived on a street of modest homes, similar to my old neighborhood. There weren't the colorful shutters of my black neighbors, but there were children playing on the sidewalks, and vegetable and flower gardens dotted the backyards.

The only distinguishing feature of the Bartlett home was a back house made of reclaimed wood. The paint on the boards didn't match; there was a stovepipe with smoke curling from it, and the dirt walkway to the structure was lined with round, concrete stepping stones. A sign over the doorway was etched in wood with the curious word "Hippocrene."

When we walked up the stairs of the main house to the front porch, I could see four rocking chairs and a small table. On it was a Bible and a glass of iced tea. Inside I noticed the neat but well-worn furniture in the living room and looked into the kitchen, where an old man was standing at the counter preparing spaghetti.

In every room, including the front porch, there was a framed picture of a Jesus with a much darker complexion than in the images I had grown up with.

"Dad, I want you to meet Cotton Mathis. He's the man I told you about who will be staying with us for a while. Cotton, everyone calls him Papa Jim."

"Nice to meet you, sir, and thanks for letting me stay here," I said as Papa Jim held out a hand with long fingers and high veins.

He took my outstretched hand in both of his and patted me. He was tall and elegant, slender, with high cheekbones, deep-set eyes, and unruly gray hair. A kitchen towel hung over his forearm. He studied my face so long that I became nervous and pretended to cough. Still, he looked at me, past my face into the black pupils of my eyes, and my whole body twitched with the discomfort of his gaze.

"Welcome, son; I didn't mean to make you uncomfortable, but everything I need to know about a person, I can see in their eyes if I look into the deep part."

I nodded to let him know I was not offended. "Why you so sad, son? What's happened to you?" Papa Jim asked.

"I'm good, sir; thanks for asking," I replied, a little rattled by his observation.

Papa Jim gave me a broad smile and pointed to the table set for three with candles and flowers. "Sit down; let's say grace."

I stood with my hand on the chair, frozen from goose bumps prickling my arms and back. Papa Jim's smile had revealed something, something we had in common, something given to me by my brother. Papa Jim had a chipped tooth, and not just any chipped tooth, it was the mirror image of my own.

"Come on, son, aren't you hungry? Let's eat," he said.

I had two helpings of spaghetti; the hot meal was a welcome change after the military food. We ate our dessert of home-made lemon-icebox pie on the porch. Papa Jim told me about his job at the Peabody Hotel, where he had waited tables for the city's elite for thirty-six years. It was a prestigious job for a black man.

"I wanted Boaz to follow me," he said. "A job at the Peabody is handed down father to son, but Boaz had other ideas. He wanted to see the world, so he joined the service; now here we are with his arm a mess and my heart broken."

"Papa, let's don't discuss this again. I'm going back when my arm is healed," said Boaz.

"Son, you don't owe them anything. There are three men still walking this earth because of you; that should be enough," Papa said.

Through dinner I had waited for an opportunity to ask Papa Jim what I really wanted to know, and now that I felt an opening, my heart was beating fast for some reason. "Sir, if you don't mind me askin', how did you get that chip in your front tooth? Have you noticed it's a lot like mine?"

"No, son, I hadn't noticed that; come over here, and let me see." I walked to the rocker where he sat and leaned over. Papa Jim took his fingers and curled back my lip, but he wasn't really looking at what was left of my tooth; he was again looking into the pupils of my eyes.

"Why, they're almost the same," he said. "My brother and I were pretty rambunctious. I don't really remember how it happened. What about yours?"

"My brother...my brother did it. He died in Vietnam a couple of years ago."

"We're real sorry to hear that, son. Boaz, you hear that? Cotton's brother didn't make it home.

"I tell him all the time that everything he needs to know about exotic places is right there in that building," Papa Jim said as he pointed to the shed in the backyard.

There was still a lazy curl of smoke rising from the stove, and I could see the flickering light of a gas lamp inside. "What do you mean, sir? What's in that building?"

"Come on, son, I'll show you the Hippocrene," said Papa Jim, and the three of us got up from our rockers to walk around to the back.

The shed had two heavy locks on the front door. It was even more rickety than it appeared from the street. When Papa Jim opened the door, the soft light from the lamp illuminated our way in. I blinked and then blinked again as I tried to understand what was before me, and then I turned in a slow circle to give myself time to sort out the breadth and depth and magic of this small space.

Here in this lowly place were more books than even our public library back home held, but they weren't organized as in a library. The books were everywhere; they filled the place like rice fills a sack. There were shelves on all four walls groaning from the weight of the books stacked in them. There were hundreds stacked all around the tiny building. Every corner, every space was filled with books. Only the stuffed chair with its flat wood arms was left uncovered, and next to it was a little table with a lamp and a stove.

When I caught my breath, I asked, "What is all this, Papa Jim?"

"I am a self-educated, erudite man, Cotton. I started reading books when my mama taught me the letters, and

I been reading ever since. I only got to the fifth grade, but that didn't stop me. I just keep reading and reading."

"Where did you get 'em all?" I asked.

"Boaz's mother, my wife, she cleaned house for a lawyer's family, and he sent me lots of them. On Saturdays, Emmaline, Boaz, and I went to thrift shops looking for used books. Cancer took Emmaline, but she's here in the books."

"They're so beautiful; I've never seen books bound like this." I picked up an exquisite copy of Dante's *Divine Comedy*. "Did the lawyer give you this?"

"Yes, he loved books too. For Christmas once, he sent Emmaline home with forty volumes of Shakespeare's complete works."

In those shelves were *The Decline and Fall of the Roman Empire*, all the writings of Thomas Jefferson and Woodrow Wilson, Civil War histories, and the collected speeches of Abraham Lincoln.

"How many books do you own, Papa Jim?" I asked.

"I lost count long ago. I've seen the Great Pyramid of Giza, the Amazon River, and the Himalayan Mountains in these books. I've read Mr. Shakespeare and Mr. Steinbeck. I've taken my picture book into the backyard and learned the constellations."

"Do people at the Peabody know about all this? Do they know how educated you are?"

"No, and it doesn't matter, son. I get a kick outta listenin' to the men I wait on. They talk about hiding their money from the government and their girlfriends from their wives. I've never once heard them speak of the Greek gods or Abraham Lincoln.

"I have something they don't," Papa Jim concluded. "I have taken a long drink from the fountain of knowledge, and they don't even know what they're missin'."

Boaz broke the spell with a yawn and said, "Come on, Dad, let's go to bed; Cotton and I have an early meeting." Papa Jim blew out the lamp and shut down the stove. He was careful to lock both the padlocks.

As we walked toward the house, my emotions were close to the surface, and Papa saw the tears coming from my eyes when we reached the light of the porch. "Why you cryin', son? Something's hurt you bad, boy. Boaz, let's sit and talk just a while longer. Cotton has something to tell us."

Listening to Papa Jim had taken my heart to places unvisited in a long time. I missed my mother who, like Emmaline, had been taken by cancer. I thought of my brother and my dad, but more than anything, I thought about my stories, those secret places, and people who had populated my childhood in the most comforting way. All I ever wanted was to write down those stories and have someone like Papa Jim love them as much as I did.

We sat on the front steps, and I told these two men I had hardly known twenty-four hours everything, all of it. I told them how I lost my family, one by one. I told them about the football days of my brother and his cowardice when it was just us two hunting for the deer. I told them how my father had been a good, hardworking man who was snakebitten by booze. I told them how when Papa Jim took my hand tonight it so reminded me of my mother's touch and the way she patted me when she went off to sleep in her sickbed.

Once I finished, I knew there was one thing more I had to confess. "Papa Jim, all my life I have wanted to write.

I want to write books, books for young men to tell them about the woods and about the great Indian hunters. I just want to write all day, every day."

Neither man said a word when I finished, and I squirmed with embarrassment for the late hour and my ramblings. "I apologize; I shouldn't have gone on and on. I feel so stupid…"

Boaz rose abruptly and said, "We've been sitting and listening to this shit for over an hour. I'm going to bed; I've heard enough."

Startled by his reaction, I said, "Oh, I've made a mess of things. I am so sorry; Sgt. Bartlett is angry with me."

Papa raised his hand for me to stop talking. "Don't pay Boaz any mind; the army has changed him. He came back from the war angry. He's hasn't drawn a happy breath since he got home, until the guard called and asked for his help. I was hopin' it would change his attitude, but I guess not. I don't want him to go back, I don't even want to think about what they'll send me home the next time.

"Cotton," Papa said softly after a long pause, "I've been waiting here for you for some time now; I knew you would come.".

"What do you mean, sir? How could that be?"

"I always knew a writer would come to the Hippocrene, someone who loved words. I knew this day would come."

"You're giving me too much credit, Papa Jim; I've never had a book published like these. My brother was the only person who ever read my stories."

"Cotton, it doesn't matter if you've written a book; you will someday. What matters is that you love words."

"Why do you call it 'the Hippocrene'?"

"In mythology, the Greek muses were the source of all knowledge and inspiration, and to them the Hippocrene spring was sacred. They believed it formed when the white-winged horse Pegasus struck the rock of Mount Helicon with his hoof. The word 'Hippocrene' means 'horse's fountain,' and it became legendary for its poetic inspiration."

"Son, I can't get your family back, but I can help you find your love of writing again," Papa Jim said. "You're welcome to spend as much time as you like in the library."

CHAPTER THIRTEEN

I dreamed of my family through the night, of the farm, and of my life in Arkansas. I had left home only a few days ago, but now it seemed a lifetime had passed. I woke early, before Boaz, and downed two cups of coffee to clear my head of last night's conversation.

Papa Jim hummed church music in the kitchen as he cooked bacon and eggs for us. Dr. King would return to Memphis in four days to make plans for the march, and once that was over, this would all be behind me.

"Mornin', Boaz," I said as I handed him a cup of coffee. He nodded, but his mood was withdrawn. We ate breakfast in silence, and I wondered if I had somehow offended him or if he was jealous that Papa had been so keen to show me the library.

Boaz finished breakfast. "Wait for me on the porch; I have a couple of calls I have to make before we leave," he said.

After ten minutes I knocked on the front door. "Come on, Boaz, we're gonna be late."

He was the first to break the silence in the car. "Why are you filling my dad's head with all that crap? He's just an old man with a bunch of books. What do you want from him? Sympathy? It's between shit and suicide in the dictionary."

"Well, actually it's not, because *y* comes after *u*."

"So you the spelling-bee champ too? How the hell with all those guardsmen did I end up with your ass, Cotton? Where did you get that stupid name anyway…you ever chopped any c-o-t-t-o-n, Cotton?"

"I didn't mean any harm, Boaz—you gotta know that. I won't say another word about the books or anything else."

"Just shut up and listen for once," he changed the subject. "I've got a job parking cars for a party at the Town and Country Club tonight. I could use an extra hand, and you could pick up some cash."

"That would be great," I said, hoping things might get better between us if I agreed to do it. "I'll need some spending money while I'm here."

"If it's not too late, there's a joint across the railroad track from the club; we could stop by there for a beer," he said.

"Sounds good," I said.

We met with the authorities at the police precinct. "Your politics get left at the door here," said the police director. "Our job is to make this city safe for Dr. King and to protect citizens and property of Memphis."

He moved to a large map of the city pinned over a chalkboard. "Each one of you has been assigned an area of downtown," he said as he called out names and pointed out assignments with a stick.

"We want you walking the streets, talking to people, going in stores and restaurants, and keeping notes on what you hear and see. You report any threats you hear and meet up with your partners at the end of the day. You're our eyes and ears in this city until this march is over and King is on that plane."

Boaz and I left the precinct and went in opposite directions: he into his familiar world, I into mine.

There were more people on the streets today. The curfew had been eased, but guardsmen were still stationed on corners and in populated areas. To me, Memphis had always been a welcoming world of music pouring from the bars on Beale Street and shoppers from three states trafficking department and specialty stores and merging with theatergoers and businessmen onto forever-bustling streets and sidewalks. But today everyone was in a hurry, with eyes on the ground and no one speaking to one another.

I shed my jacket. I was burning up. It started with my feet and worked its way up until I could feel my face heating to a bright red. My hands were shaking. The confessions I had made to Papa Jim last night played over and over in my head.

I walked up the street past Goldsmith's Department Store to the Planters Peanuts stall. A small crowd gathered around, eating the warm peanuts from white greasy sacks.

"Nice day, huh?" I said to the man next to me in line. "I don't know about you, but I'm glad they've lifted the curfew. What do you think about this mess?"

"What I think is none of your business," the man shot back, and with that the stall owner told me to move along.

Dejected, I walked a block, sat on a bus bench, and tried to think of a simpler way to pick up conversations.

I looked around. Across the street was a small barn with a sign that read The Green Beetle Bar and Grill. Two doors opened to the street, but somehow the place was still dark inside. I took a seat at the lunch counter with a good view of the sidewalk. A sign in the window advertised the best-grilled cheese in town. It was too early for lunch, but a beer sounded really good.

I wasn't the only man in Memphis who needed a drink. Bars had been closed since the riots, and this was the Beetle's first day open since the curfew. I took a seat at one end of the counter looking out onto the sidewalk. A priest sat drinking a glass of iced tea at the other end of the counter. I ordered a beer.

The priest moved down to the stool next to me. "You from Memphis?" he asked. He had a large reddened face that might have been affected by the tightness of his clerical collar. His thinning hair was gray.

"No, only visiting for a few days; just my luck to get caught in a riot. What do ya think about all this?"

"I'm in the business of saving souls same as Dr. King," he said. "He's a well-meaning man, but people don't change without a fight. We'll all be glad when this is over."

"If you don't mind me askin', what's a man of God doin' in a bar at eleven in the morning?" I asked.

"No better place than a bar to find lost souls. Do you know God?"

"I'm good. Thanks, Reverend," I said.

"Good to hear." He patted me on the back and moved on to a more willing lost soul.

It was close to noon when I ordered the second beer, and by then the place was jammed with businessmen eating cheese sandwiches and downing double vodkas, so the smell of liquor wouldn't accompany them back to the office. There were construction workers who had sneaked in for a beer during lunch and beleaguered men who had spent too much time cooped up with their wives during the curfew. Even though no one was speaking to one other on the street, there was plenty of talk in here.

"That troublemaker needs to go back to Atlanta and leave us alone; everything was fine until he showed up," the man next to me said.

"He's just usin' us for his own gain. He wants the publicity for the poor-folks rally he's plannin' in Washington. We're just a convenient way for him to get his face on the TV," the bartender shot back.

"You think there's gonna be trouble when he comes back in a couple of days?" I asked.

"There won't be trouble at my house," the bartender said. "I already got my two rifles and handgun outta the safe."

"We'da worked out this integration thing in time if these outsiders had stayed outta of our business," said a man from across the room.

"I'm gonna keep my kids outta school while he's here. We're taking shifts in my neighborhood to protect ourselves," the bartender said.

This was exactly the information I needed to take back to the precinct this afternoon. I ordered a couple of more beers while I listened to the conversations around me.

"That Loeb's got it right for once; he can't give in to that union."

"Yeah, that Yankee union guy is makin' a fool of his greasy self."

"If there's another riot, we've got to protect ourselves; all my guns are loaded."

I had always been able to hold my liquor well; besides, I was feeling better, less anxious. The afternoon wore on, with the priest and myself sizing up everyone who came into the bar for our own purposes. When I left for my meeting with Boaz, the priest had cornered a crying drunk in the back booth.

Boaz had selected a rooming house across the street from the Lorraine Motel as our meeting place. Dr. King and his associates often stayed at the motel on trips to Memphis. The newspaper had criticized King for holing up in the more expensive Rivermont Tower after the riot, so it was a good bet he would stay at the Lorraine on his return visit.

I got to the rooming house first. An afternoon of drinking had made me foggy on last night's confessions, but I remembered now, and my hands were shaking again.

When Boaz arrived, we went into the rooming house; it smelled dank, the carpets were moldy, and the walls were painted a disgusting pea-soup green. There was a large, frumpy woman at the front desk. Her face was swollen, and her left eye had a blue mark under it that looked like the remnants of a recent beating. She wore a flowered, frilly blouse that looked out of character, and on it was a name tag that read Bessie.

"Bessie, I wonder if we could speak with you in private," Boaz said.

"That's Miss Bessie to you; whatcha need?"

"We're with the police."

"Let's go in my office," she said.

Boaz explained our assignment to her, and she agreed we could meet there in her office in the afternoons and use the phone to call in our reports.

"I don't want any trouble, and you have the police watch my building, you hear?"

She left us alone to call in our report. "There's a lot of fear out there; my people are pretty scared, and the newspaper isn't helping," Boaz said. My account of the afternoon at the bar didn't make him feel much better. He phoned the police to discuss our findings, and we headed back to Papa Jim's to clean up before going to the country club. I needed more than a shower; I needed time to sober up.

Boaz was polishing his car when I met him in the driveway. We drove through parts of Memphis I had never seen, and when we turned onto the street where the Town and Country Club was located, for the first time the shiny Chevy car seemed like a clunker.

I had never seen homes like these; most of the mansions had a golf course as their backyard. There were gardeners working the grounds and dozens of maids in black dresses with white aprons ambling to the bus stop after a long day's work. There were no children outside playing, and high wrought-iron fences with gates surrounded most of the properties.

"How many people live in these houses? Are they apartment buildings?" I asked Boaz, and he laughed.

"No, man, just one family lives in them. They're somethin', aren't they?" he said.

The club occupied a full city block. The golf course was built in the 1930s, and the fairways were shaded with ancient oaks. The clubhouse was two stories and white with black shutters. There were eight columns across the front porch. The only entrance was through a guard gate.

"Boaz, I don't know about this. I've never been around people like this," I said.

"You'll be fine."

"This place gives me the creeps. What if I wreck one of the cars? The only thing I've ever driven is a pickup."

Boaz pulled into the guard gate, and the guard reached through the window to shake his hand. "Your daddy just stopped by to tell me you were comin'; you fellas go 'round back."

The warm greeting from the guard didn't make me feel any better. My hands were shaking more than before.

We entered through the kitchen door, and one of the waiters handed us jackets that read "Parking" on the front pocket.

"There he is, our hero," shouted one of the kitchen staff. "Come in here, and let us get a look at you. How's that arm?"

Boaz was swarmed by the buzz of the club employees as they gathered to greet him. "How's those grandchildren of yours?" Boaz asked a friend.

"Your wife outta the hospital yet?" he asked, putting his arm around the shoulders of an older man.

While Boaz spoke with his admirers, I walked through the double swinging doors of the kitchen and peered into the dining room. The tables were set with cloths of lace. The staff were lighting candles in tall, silver holders. The china was rimmed in dark blue and gold.

An orchestra was warming up at the back of the room, and there were lights that twitched off and on, in a soft rhythm with the music. There was a lady directing the staff. She had on a beautiful coral dress with a full skirt, and her blond hair was swept high. Four tuxedoed men were laughing among themselves in a corner of the room. Silk curtains covered all the windows.

The waiter led us to the portico where we would be stationed. "Snap to it when these cars come in. They like to see you runnin'; you'll get better tips. Be respectful, especially to the women. You give the driver a card with a number. Here they come; pull your shoulders back."

I was beginning to sober up. "Boaz, I'm not so sure about this."

"Too late now; open the car door for that lady, let's go."

Gleaming sedans pulled under the portico as Boaz and I worked the line and moved the cars to the rear parking lot. He was right: we were on a dead run just to keep up with the crowd.

I had started to get my rhythm after about a half hour when a white Cadillac convertible with a red interior pulled in, just as we were running back from the lot. It was brand new and still had the drive-out tags from the dealer. It looked like a winged chariot with its long sleek lines and fins on the back. I was mesmerized; I had never seen anything as beautiful until out of the back seat of that car came an even more beautiful vision in a sapphire-blue evening dress.

She had auburn hair that swung sweetly on her bare back and shoulders. I held my hand out to help her from the car, and when she looked up at me, I could see there was nothing sweet about her. This girl was looking for trouble. She held her gaze at me far too long, put a tight squeeze on my hand, and then looked back and winked as she headed for the steps.

From behind, a booming male voice shouted, "Get in that club, Corinne!" And then he addressed Boaz, "Get over here, boy; I would rather have a nigger take my car than this lecherous idiot."

He turned to me and sneered, "Son, I should get you fired."

"I didn't do anything, and don't call him that. This man is a war hero," I shouted back.

Boaz pulled me back by the collar and jumped in the car to take it to the lot. "Sorry, sir, we'll get it taken care of for you." To me, he said, "Don't do that, Cotton; just keep your mouth shut. It'll only make things worse."

I was still angry when all the cars had been parked. I took the key to the Cadillac and walked back to the lot. I opened the car door and sat for a moment admiring all the gadgets, and I put it in neutral and turned up the radio. After listening to a couple of songs, I stood up and took a long satisfying piss on the driver's side seat.

We collected our money, and Boaz pointed across the tracks to his favorite club, The Outrigger. Even on this weeknight, the parking lot was jammed.

"We gotta get up early, man; I'm not feelin' so good," I said.

"Oh, come on, just a beer or two won't hurt," he said. "Not a lot of white people there, but stay with me and you'll be all right."

It was close to midnight when we walked through the door and heard the strains of Memphis native Rufus Thomas's song "Walking the Dog." A few stares followed our walk to the bar, but I didn't feel threatened. Boaz had friends here too. We got our beers and found a table. Boaz worked the room, greeting people, and he pointed me out to his friends from across the room.

I ordered another beer for us. Boaz walked back to our table. "Music's pretty good, huh? I'm goin' to the men's room; be back in a minute."

I was watching the dance floor when, from behind me, I felt a tap on my shoulder. It was a girl Boaz had spoken with, and she was lovely.

She smiled in a coy way. "Would you like to dance?"

"Sure." She took my hand, and the crowd parted when we walked onto the floor.

She was a great dancer. She whispered in my ear, "You like black women?"

"I like women in general."

"You gotta car?"

"No," I begged off, feeling uncomfortable with the patron's stares, "I've got to find Boaz; we have to be up early for work. Thanks for the dance."

I looked for Boaz, and I walked in the direction of the men's room to find him. Maybe he had run into an old friend there.

I didn't see the man coming from the shadows. He went for my gut. The force knocked me to the ground, and when I finally got my footing, he rammed a pipe against my neck and slammed me into the wall. I couldn't breathe, and I felt my knees go weak underneath me.

With my popping eyes, I could see Boaz at the end of the hallway. He just stood there watching me gasp, close to fainting. He turned and walked away, didn't even look back. I somehow found the strength to knee the bastard in the groin. The pipe dropped, and I left him writhing on the floor.

Crazed, I ran through the club, shouting for Boaz, and someone pointed outside. I caught him in the parking lot and pushed him into his car. "What the hell was that, man, what the hell was that?"

"Get in the car, Cotton. We have to be at work in the morning."

The next morning, I was still fuming. Papa had left for work before we were up, and Boaz and I had coffee and toast in silence. We didn't speak to one another on the ride downtown. The car never made a full stop before I jumped out near the rooming house.

Miss Bessie was behind the counter in the same flowered blouse, and she was puffing on a cigarette.

"I need a room here until Dr. King's march is over. The city will pay for it."

She led me down a dark hallway, smelling of vomit from some drunk the night before. It was on the third floor. There was only one bathroom for the six rooms on the floor, and the mattress was thin, but still it was better than having to spend one more minute in the home of Boaz Bartlett.

I walked across the street to The Green Beetle, where I would start and end the day's surveillance. The place was empty except for the priest drinking his tea and the bartender.

"Mornin', Reverend, saved any souls yet today?"

"No, son, but I'm beginning to worry about you. You look terrible, and if you're in town for just a few days, I could suggest some things to do other than sit in a bar all day. What are you up to here?"

"You don't worry about me. I'll take care of my business, and you take care of the Lord's. We understand each other?" The priest moved to the back of the bar and waited for his next prospect.

I decided to switch from beer to vodka and had three with tonic before noon. Later I walked the streets in a drunken haze. I didn't meet Boaz at our scheduled time, but I did make it to the precinct for a four o'clock briefing. I had nothing to add to the discussion.

I caught up with Boaz after the meeting. "If you need me, I'm staying at the rooming house. I'll pick up my things later today. I'm gonna finish this job and collect my check; then I'm getting the hell out of Memphis."

"The further away you stay from me, the better," Boaz called after me.

I bought a bottle on the way to the rooming house and went to bed early. The next day was a repeat of the day before.

The steady drinking of vodka was lifting my anger enough that I began to think I could make it through this ordeal. For two days Boaz and I met in the rooming-house office, made our report, and went our separate ways. He never made any effort to reconcile. At night I drank until I passed out.

On the morning of April 3, I woke in a drunken haze. It was the day Dr. King was scheduled to return to Memphis. Though the march was still five days away, he was to arrive early for planning sessions. This would soon be over.

At our early-morning briefing, the precinct had a sense of urgency. There were law-enforcement personnel from every local authority and at least seventy-five FBI men.

"This is it, fellas. Dr. King is back today, and we are on the highest possible alert. I don't care how small it seems— if you hear anything, let us know," the director said.

The FBI man in charge of Memphis operations had a very serious tone. "The city is going to file an injunction to stop the march. Once Dr. King arrives, he will be in meetings all day. He'll be in the City Hall area until late this afternoon."

I didn't understand the legal wrangling, but I had learned enough since arriving in Memphis to know that Dr. King would be committed to staging that march. There wouldn't be any action in my assigned area until later in the day, so I bought a vodka pint, stuck it in my jacket pocket, and settled on a bus bench overlooking the river.

CHAPTER FOURTEEN

As Dr. King headed to the Atlanta airport for his return trip to Memphis on the morning of April 3, he was nursing a cold, on top of everything else with which he had to concern himself.

The day was made worse as the plane idled at the gate for over an hour. When it finally pushed off, the pilot spoke through the intercom to say they were being delayed because Dr. Martin Luther King was aboard and that every piece of luggage was being checked to ensure the plane's safety. Unsettled already with what Memphis might hold for him, the reverend shot a worried glance at his advisors.

Met not only by Memphis police, FBI, and local ministers, Dr. King was greeted with blustery winds; bloated, low-hanging clouds; and a tornado watch. There was to be the threat of thunderstorms all day.

The Lorraine Motel was central in location to the Clayborn and Mason Temples and Beale Street, which were centerpieces of the garbage strike. The motel was a two-story cinderblock structure that was owned and operated by a black couple who took great pride in their business. There were home-cooked meals and warm greetings for return customers. Dr. King had stayed at the Lorraine several times, and today he was given his favorite room number, 306, which was made known to any interested party, as the door and number were pictured on local evening-news broadcasts. The balcony to his room overlooked a courtyard and a swimming pool, as yet unopened for the season. He was eating in the motel dining room when marshals arrived with the injunction in hand. Dr. King had a pleasant response for everyone involved. This was a legal maneuver he had battled many times. Local lawyers were assembled to fight the injunction, and Dr. King wearily headed to work with his associates.

Edmund Orgill's old friend, Attorney Lucius Burch, still walked the halls of Memphis courtrooms and advocated for liberal causes. He was less naïve now than in his younger days, when he had backed Orgill for mayor, but he was the perfect choice to appeal to the court that the garbagemen and their supporters should be allowed to march. After meeting with King, Burch knew the civil-rights leader believed that the redemption march was King's last chance to revive his damaged career.

Plainclothes Memphis police officers had watched King's every move since his plane hit the ground. From a perch inside Memphis Firehouse No. 2, located just across the street from the Lorraine Motel, they watched the comings and goings of the reverend and his staff through a newspaper-covered window, with small slits cut for viewing outside with their binoculars. They saw his staff and his confidantes. There were a documentary filmmaker and a *New York Times* reporter. Later they would watch as King's brother and lady friend would make a dramatic entrance in a baby-blue Cadillac convertible.

King was exhausted from the day of meetings. Ill with a cold, he begged off the planned rally at Mason Temple that night, asking Abernathy to deliver a speech in his absence. Tornado warnings were out, and by the time the storm passed, twelve people would be dead and at least a hundred injured.

As the afternoon wore on, the weather worsened. When thunder rolls across the Mississippi River from Arkansas, it can have a low rumble that sounds like God clearing his throat. Once the thunder collides with the water, the sound rises above the bluffs of Memphis and can explode with a *bam* like the simultaneous slam of a thousand doors. Late in that day of April 3, 1968, the thunder rolled; God slammed the door and thrust the back of Memphis into a wall. Within twenty-four hours, God would move on, but Memphis would be mired for decades in the muck left from that miserable storm.

When Abernathy reached the meeting hall, he was surprised to find three thousand people; they had braved the rain and left families at home to suffer through the storm, and many were from the Public Works Department. He felt the weight of their loss if King did not appear. Abernathy called King at the Lorraine and told him about the crowd, and King relented.

Even though it was nine o'clock by the time King arrived, other speakers had kept the audience warm, and

Abernathy took an unusual amount of time introducing King. For twenty-five minutes, he eulogized Dr. King's path from the cradle to the moment of their standing at Mason Temple. Outside, the storm continued with such force, and the windows high in the building rattled so loud Abernathy could hardly be heard at times. King was perspiring, and, to some on the podium, he looked wan.

Dr. King rose from his chair and plugged into the crowd, hoping their enthusiasm would fire his engines. He started in low tones and built his case: "Something is happening in Memphis. Something is happening in our world."

He brought the audience to the beginning of time and told them that, if given a choice, he would still want to be a man of the latter half of the twentieth century. He continued with: "Trouble is in the land, confusion is all around... but only when it is dark enough, you can see the stars."

Bam, bam, bam went the shutter from the windows high above, as the wind wailed and thunder shook the church.

He urged the rapt audience to continue the struggles brought on by the strike, to have concern for their brothers and rise up together.

He spoke of Jesus and of the Good Samaritan. He told the people about his morning plane ride and the threats on his life. He described the scene in a Harlem store when a deranged woman had attacked him with a letter opener. The blade had almost punctured his aorta. Doctors told him had he but sneezed, he would have drowned in his own blood.

He warned the days ahead would be difficult and conceded that his own longevity was in the hands of God. He shared the grace of his future vision: to see his flock make it over the mountain and see the Promised Land.

He ended with: "So I am happy tonight. I'm not worried about anything. I'm fearing no man," and he shouted to the glory of the coming of the Lord.

The audience rose with a thunder that challenged God's storm that day. In their hope for a better America, their decades of frustration poured forth to winch up this weary man, and King fell in his seat with tears welling in his eyes. Many others were openly weeping. No one wanted to leave.

King was buoyant when he left Mason Temple with associates. One reported, "He's preached the fear out..."

It was close to midnight when King arrived at the home of a friend. The storm had passed, and there was unexpected good news. Reverend A. D. King, Dr. King's younger brother, while driving from Florida back to his home in Louisville, Kentucky, had decided on an impulse to make a detour to Memphis and see his brother. With him was Dr. King's lady friend, a state senator from Kentucky.

CHAPTER FIFTEEN

As I made my way into the Memphis city streets on the morning of April 4, city workers were picking up downed tree branches and leaves from the previous night's storm. If people in downtown Memphis were aware of the pending march or legal wrangling, an outsider would have never noticed it. Commerce was transacted with no signs of fear or trepidation. The streets were once again bustling.

I planned to spend the morning in Goldsmith's Department Store, have lunch at The Green Beetle, and then spend the afternoon there. I was to meet Boaz at five-thirty in the afternoon and would walk with him to our daily briefing at the police station. In the past few days, we had managed to keep our conversations on police business, nothing else; it was tolerable for me.

That same morning, just outside the Memphis city limits and across the state line in Mississippi, a man checked out of a seedy motel and bought a Memphis newspaper. Printed on the paper's front page was a photograph of Dr. King standing in front of room number 306 of the Lorraine Motel. The man got into a white Ford Mustang and headed north for the Tennessee border.

⇥ ⇤

The walk from the rooming house to Goldsmith's was about six blocks. The wind was swirling so much that I had small pieces of debris in both my eyes as the storm front still persecuted the atmosphere on its way out of town.

A peculiar *clunk, clunk, clunk* sound became louder and louder as I walked toward the river and the store. *Clunk... clunk, clunk, clunk.* It was deafening. People walked along with their hands cupped to their ears. *Clunk, clunk, clunk.* I discovered the source of the clamor when I reached the corner across the street from Goldsmith's.

In the bell tower of the Methodist church, workers were frantically trying to save the church bell, which had been a victim of the storm.

"Hold on to it, hold on; we need to get these ropes around it," one of the men shouted to the others.

Clunk, clunk, clunk. It clanged as the men attempted to tie ropes on the enormous bell that was now hanging on one side over the tower.

The minister stood below, looking up at the men; he was concerned for their safety and for the bell. He shouted, "Be careful up there. We don't want anyone to get hurt."

I stood and watched as they tied the ropes and worked together to pull the bell back into place.

Clunk, clunk, clunk...thud. People on the street gasped in horror as one of the men was catapulted to the sidewalk when the errant bell was struck by a sudden wind gust. The minister rushed to the man's side, but he was already dead, deep in a pool of blood from his cracked skull.

I turned and ran, ran as fast as I could run back from where I had come and ducked from the street into the safety of The Green Beetle.

"I just saw a man die," I said to the bartender.

"You what?"

"I just saw a man die; he fell from the bell tower on the Methodist Church."

Before I could say more, sirens came screaming from every direction on the way to the scene.

"Give me a double vodka tonic."

⊨⊹ ⊹⊨

The man in the white Mustang arrived in Memphis late in the morning. He spent an hour driving around and around the blocks of buildings and stores that adjoined the Lorraine Motel. He finally settled on the rooming house across the street from the motel. He parked his car in front and smiled as he confirmed the rooming house had a direct line of sight to the Lorraine.

He opened the door to the rooming house and stepped into the office of Miss Bessie, the manager. Her hair was rolled in pink curlers, and she wore her favorite loose-fitting flowered blouse with ruffles.

"Got any vacancies?" the man asked.

⊨⊹ ⊹⊨

It took two drinks before my hands were no longer shaky and I could breathe at a normal rate. The regular group of businessmen and construction workers rolled in around noon to have their grilled cheese and afternoon cocktail.

"Did you hear about the poor fella who fell off the church this mornin'?" the man next to me said to all of us at the bar.

The bartender was wiping the counter and looked at me. I said nothing.

"Yeah, poor sap got knocked off by the bell. It happened so fast he never knew what hit him."

I ordered another drink. The bartender put a sandwich in front of me even though I had not ordered it.

From the back of the room, someone said, "That storm was somethin'. My wife and kids were scared to death last night."

I ate the sandwich. Just hearing voices, even of people I did not know, made me feel a little better, more normal. The chatter continued, but there was no mention of King's return to Memphis today.

The lunch crowd was gone within an hour, back to their regular lives. I envied them. It was only then I noticed the Catholic priest in the back booth. His head was cradled in his arms, and he looked asleep.

"Is he all right?" I asked the bartender and nodded back toward the priest.

"He'll be fine; he's just off the wagon again. It hasn't happened for a couple of months, but when it does, it's bad."

"You mean he's a drunk?"

"Yeah, for a long time. The Catholics kicked him out of his parish years ago, so he just walks the streets and comes in here every day. I'll let him sleep it off at my place tonight."

That was enough for me; nothing in this town was as it seemed. It was close to 2:00 p.m., still hours before I was to meet Boaz. I paid my tab and walked back into the swirling wind. The streets were wet, and leaves were flying through the air. It was early spring, so the trees had not yet leafed out and the city still had that barren, winter palette.

Miss Bessie was accustomed to all sorts of derelicts and losers coming through the rooming house, but this guy was different. He was slender and clean-shaven, and wore a dark suit and tie. He looked at her through beady, dark eyes, but she shook off her premonitions and decided he was just an ordinary businessman.

"Will you just be here for the night?" she asked.

"No, I'll pay you in advance for a week's stay," he replied.

She showed him her nicest room and told him the price would be $10.50 for the week. It had a kitchenette and was clean.

The man looked around. "What else you got?"

She led him up the stairs to the second floor. The room had a broken doorknob, and there was a bare lightbulb and a filthy red couch. Plaster had fallen from the ceiling, leaving the wood exposed. She didn't mention that the last tenant of the room had died there.

The man paid no attention to the sorry conditions; his attention was on the view from the one window in the room. It had a direct line of sight to the Lorraine Motel.

"This'll do just fine," he said.

I wandered back in the direction of Goldsmith's. Between the vodka and the wind, I was having a hard time walking in a straight line. I passed the Methodist Church, and the only evidence of the morning's tragedy was the still-dangling bell swaying in the tower. Even the blood on the sidewalk had been cleaned away.

Inside the department store I watched crowds ride up and down the escalator. There was nothing unusual going on here, just mothers and children, retired people and laughing teenagers out for a day of shopping. If I went back to the rooming house, I would have time for a nap before the meeting. There was nothing of interest to report on the streets today. A nap would do me good.

⇥⊹ ⊹⇤

The man surveyed his room and decided to move a dresser away from the window to get a better line of sight to the Lorraine Motel. Across the street he saw the baby-blue Cadillac that Dr. King's lover and his brother had arrived in during last night's storm.

The man calculated that room number 306 was about two hundred feet away from and about twelve feet below his perch. There was a problem, however. He would have to lean far out of the window to get the exact line of sight he desired.

He walked down the hall to the communal bathroom and found the angle from its window to be much more satisfactory; from there, a mere crack in the window would suit his purposes.

⇥⊹ ⊹⇤

About halfway back to the rooming house, I passed a young boy wearing a yarmulke, resting on the back of his head. His father was dressed in the manner of an Orthodox Jew, all in black with a heavy beard and tall black hat. The boy was walking a small white dog on a leash.

"Let's cross the street here, son," the man said.

The boy jumped the curb into the street, and when he did, the leash dropped out of his hand. The little dog bolted into the street straight into the path of an oncoming taxi. The taxi driver never even bothered to stop after he hit the dog.

"Father, Father, help me, help me. I didn't mean to let go," the boy cried out.

I watched horrified as the man and the boy rushed into the street and held the little dog, which died in the boy's arms.

The father cradled the boy as the child wailed and cried.

Something was happening in Memphis. Something was happening in my world. It was troubling and confusing, and I couldn't stay here any longer. I would tell the authorities this afternoon that I was leaving. The money no longer meant enough for me to stay.

I stopped at a pay phone and dialed Booker's number. I needed to hear a voice from home.

"Hell-o."

"Booker," I said, "it's Cotton. I just needed to talk to you."

"Where are you, boy?"

"I'm in Memphis. I took a job here for a few days. It pays good, but I'm comin' home. I'm gonna call Froggie tonight, and he'll come get me."

"Sounds good. What kinda job? Memphis is in a mess right now."

"I'll tell you 'bout it when I see you. Will you and Sallie be at your place this weekend?"

"Same as always, you come see us."

"Booker?"

"Yeah, Cotton, what is it?"

"What about Dewdrop—is he okay?"

"He's fine; you come see for yourself."

I hung up the phone and went in the direction of the rooming house. The sound of my steps reminded me of an Alfred Hitchcock movie; they were distinct and heavy on the pavement. I couldn't wait to get out of this town, but there was one thing I had left to do. I had to settle the score with Boaz. I had to find out what had caused him to betray me, the source of his anger with me, even if I had to beat it out of him.

When I got back to the rooming house, it was 4:00 p.m. I had an hour and a half before I was to meet Boaz, and I needed the time to think about what I would say.

I took the stairs, two at time, to my second-floor room. At the top of the stairs was a man I had not seen before. He looked out of place; he was dressed in a dark business suit and had a serious look on his face. I wondered if he was a G-man with the FBI.

⟢ ⟣

The man walked down the stairs of the rooming house into the light of the Memphis streets. The clouds had broken open to the sun, but the wind was still swirling.

He drove his white Mustang the short distance to the York Arms Sporting Goods store. The store had been looted during the riots, and the owner was there still trying to make things right again on the shelves.

"You got any binoculars? I need some with that night vision in them," the man said.

"Don't have any with night vision, but I have a really nice pair here. They were made in Japan," the shop owner replied.

The man tried out the binoculars and took a roll of bills from his pocket. He drove back to the rooming house about 4:30 p.m. and parked the Mustang some distance from the rooming house. He noticed two women standing at the window of the Seabrook Paint and Wallpaper store. The women saw the man in the Mustang, too; they thought, like themselves, he was waiting for someone. It was close to five o'clock when the women left. The man opened his trunk, took out a long box, and wrapped it inside an old, green bedspread, along with the new binoculars. He went through the door of the rooming house and climbed the stairs to his room.

Memphis police officers were beginning to gather and compare notes for the upcoming meeting. At the nearby fire station, two policemen with binoculars traded shifts and peered through a hole in a newspaper that was taped to a window. The locker-room window of the station had a clear view to the Lorraine Motel, and there had been constant surveillance there since King returned to Memphis the day before.

Through the day they had observed King and his group joking, laughing, and conferring with the lawyers. Dr. King had a late lunch of fried catfish and then was ready for a nap. He had been pacing the floor, waiting to hear the outcome of the court decision concerning the march, and it was beginning to sap his energy.

The Memphis police officers were not the only ones with eyes trained on the Lorraine Motel at that moment. The man in rooming house number 5B picked up his new binoculars and set his sights to look up to the second floor of the motel across the street.

I lay on my bed and planned what I would say to Boaz. I knew I was making the right decision to leave Memphis. I had some money saved, and that would get me by until my next paycheck from the farm. I would tell the National Guard commander I had completed most of my assignment but that I needed to return home for personal reasons. It was less than an hour before Boaz would arrive at the rooming house. The more I watched the clock, the more my hands shook.

CHAPTER SIXTEEN

Finally, late in the afternoon, the lawyers arrived at the Lorraine Motel. Now King's mood lifted as the lawyers bragged about the skillful way Lucius Burch had handled the proceedings. The march would go forth on the coming Monday with strict guidelines, but they had won.

What Martin Luther King stood for depended on the observer. To his supporters, he was the student of Gandhi, convinced that nonviolence was the most potent force of protection offered by the universe. To his enemies, his benevolence in the face of scorn served to incite violence in others while King stood back and took no responsibility. But in his daily life, his vulnerability served as motivation, not fear. No one around him was allowed to be armed. There were no bodyguards; he never requested police protection. Even his own children were not allowed to play with toy guns.

A special tactical unit of the Memphis Police Department came into the firehouse a few minutes before six. They had been monitoring the marchers through another uneventful day. A dozen of them were joking and having coffee with the on-duty firemen.

"Well, the order just came back: the judge is gonna allow this damn march," said one of the policemen.

"God, I pray that preacher gets out of town without any more trouble," someone in the room responded.

The patrolman assigned to watch through the window was at the end of his shift. He fought to keep his attention on his binoculars, which were trained on room 306.

Inside room 306, Reverend King and his beloved friend Ralph Abernathy were playing out a scene that had been perfected in countless hotel rooms for thirteen years. King was running late as Abernathy coaxed him along, and King was enjoying the coaxing. It was an amusement King used to relax as he performed his elaborate shaving routine, whose smell ran most associates out of the room. *The Huntley-Brinkley Report* could be heard from the television.

The group was invited for a soul-food feast at the home of a prominent Memphis minister, Billy Kyles, and his wife. King joked about how pretty Mrs. Kyles was and how he was going to primp especially for her. He feigned that his tie was lost when it was on the chair in his direct sight. At five minutes to six, the three men walked out of the door onto the motel balcony. Reverend Kyles teased King about his expanding waistline.

Outside, spring sent a promise after the storm, with mild temperatures and a breeze coming from the Mississippi River. The Memphis skyline lights began to appear in early evening, and King beamed as he thought about the day's victory. Earlier, back in the room, he had mentioned to friends how much that first speech in Memphis had meant to him.

He said it felt like the early, enthusiastic days of the civil-rights movement. He was so pleased that he had followed his instincts and, rather than listening to his advisers, had agreed to allow these lowly garbagemen to lift him from his recent malaise. The riot was unfortunate, but in a few days, his message of peace would again circulate on the airways.

On the balcony King took a pen and wrote a note to himself for an upcoming speech. The note said, "Nothing is gained without sacrifice." He leaned over the balcony to speak to associates. Dr. King's lady friend put the finishing touches on her hair as she listened to the banter outside her door. Two of the men were playfully shadowboxing one another.

Dr. King was introduced to a musician who was standing in the courtyard below. His band had come from Chicago to play at the Mason Temple tonight to support the strikers.

King said to him, "I want you to sing for me tonight at the meeting. I want you to do that song, 'Take My Hand, Precious Lord.' I want you to sing it like you've never sung it before. Sing it *real* pretty."

⇥⇤

The man in the rooming house had just gotten the sights set on his binoculars when, at 5:55 p.m., Dr. King and his group came walking onto the motel balcony. The man had been tracking King for months and yearning to confront him, and now he had just come sauntering out into the open within five minutes into this watch. In a panic, the man calculated a better sight line was probably from the communal bathroom just down the hall. He grabbed the green bedspread and his glasses and ran the short distance down the hall. He slammed the bathroom door shut and locked it.

CHAPTER SEVENTEEN

Just before five-thirty, I went down the stairs of the rooming house to wait for Boaz. I saw Dr. King and several of his associates across the street at the Lorraine Motel, talking on the balcony. I knew the binoculars of the police were trained on them from their perch in the firehouse.

The wind was no longer swirling, just a gentle breeze, and, in fact, the street was eerily quiet. The storm of the night before was over, and I looked toward the river where, earlier in the day, I had witnessed two deaths.

For an hour and a half, I had been in my room going back over every detail of the attack in the Outrigger Bar and Boaz's betrayal. Why did he leave me there with a pipe against my throat when I had just stood up for him at the country club?

From the Outrigger incident, I descended into a rabbit hole of self-pity. Why was my family not like Timbo's family? Why was my brother so talented at football when I was the one who could have made the tough plays and won the game? Why did my mother have to die? Was I responsible for my father's suicide?

The furnace of smoldering anger inside me was stoked by vodka. I took one last swill, and, with it, something inside me swelled and spurt forth with a primal scream.

The shabby, threadbare room was no match for the roil of my temper, which was as muddied by the sediment of my miserable life as the brown and swirling Mississippi River. The mattress curled on the floor as I threw it against the wall, and pillows ripped open with the force of my beatings. Three times I attacked the wall, until my hand was bloodied and the gaping hole I made exposed mice hiding inside, who ran about the room in terror. By the time I reached the street, my face was red with rage and dripping with sweat, and my jaw was clenched.

It was from this moment, on the sidewalk outside the house as I waited for Boaz, that everything in my life became like thousands of sequential photographic images. When I remember, and I can remember it all in detail, the memories are accompanied with the sound of clipped clicks of a camera.

When Boaz rounded the corner and we came face to face on the sidewalk, he could see something in me had changed.

He stepped back away from me a bit and spoke in a low voice from the back of his throat as he began to go over the daily report, "The minister at Mason Temple is asking for more police protection during the march. I think it's a good idea."

Across Main Street the garbage workers were there with their placards that read "I AM A MAN." Pedestrians made a path around them and kept to their business without expression. When I raised my voice, they looked in our direction.

"Just *what's* the problem, Boaz? What have I done to you?" I asked and jabbed his shoulder back with my hand.

"Are you drunk, man?"

"I asked you, what's the problem?" I said.

"Cotton, let's just get through this; we don't ever have to see each other again when this is over," Boaz said.

"I'm not leavin' Memphis until I know."

"Know what?"

"Why you set me up; why you turned your back on me."

The street's silence was broken by laughter coming from the motel balcony where Dr. King and his friends shouted back and forth at one another in a lighthearted way.

Boaz gave no answer; he only stared at the ground.

"Huh?" I took both hands and rammed them into his shoulders. Still, he did not look at me.

"Tell me, tell me now!" I screamed at him. The strikers stopped their slow, circular pace; put down their placards; and stared at the two of us and the commotion. When Boaz still did not answer, they took up their signs and resumed their demonstration.

"I knew your brother...in Vietnam," Boaz said.

"You what? How could you have known my brother?" I was dumbfounded.

"He was in my regiment; I watched him die. He deserved to die," he said, still not looking at me. "I *hated him*. We all hated him!" I stepped back, made a fist, and took a hard swing at Boaz, but he was too well-trained, too fast for me. He blocked my hit with his forearm.

"Who do you think you are, nigger? You can't talk like that about him. What did he do to you? What does that have to do with me?" I shouted.

Two police cars drove by, slowed to watch the strikers for a moment, and then went in the direction of the river.

"It's almost six; we have to call in the report, Cotton. We'll talk about this later, cm'on. And don't call me 'nigger,' you white honky, and I mean it."

"We're not going anywhere until you tell me what you know," I said.

"Didn't the army tell you what happened? Your loser of a brother couldn't get a shot off."

"Yeah," I said, "but what the hell does that have to do with me? I'm not my brother. Why would you double-cross *me*?"

"Because I hate you too," he said with tears streaming down his face. He was trembling. "Because he's like the spit in my throat; I can't get rid of him, and now I can't get rid of you." The war hero, the man with the mangled arm and the decorated chest, dropped to the curb and sobbed like a schoolboy.

"I'm not my brother, Boaz," I shouted. The strikers once again looked our way. "I can take a shot; don't test me."

As that witches' brew of past and present, stirred to poison my future, I could have killed Boaz; I wanted to kill Boaz, but Boaz was saved by a blast from above, a gunshot from a window in the rooming house.

Even though I had spent my childhood in the woods, the sound of that rifle was like nothing I had ever heard before. In hunting the discharge provokes a suspended split second when the animal wonders, will the bullet hit or won't it? The blast I heard at 6:01 p.m. was a rushing roar of evil. This bullet had a death wish and would accept nothing less from its target.

"That was a gun; they've shot at King!" I tried to pull Boaz up from the curb, but he refused and fell with his head in his hands.

"I can't, I can't, you go," he sobbed.

I raced inside the rooming house and screamed for Miss Bessie in the lobby. A loud clamor came from the staircase. The man in the dark suit, the man I had seen at the top of the stairs earlier, flew out of the door with a green blanket tucked under his arm.

I chased him through the door as he bolted and scattered the strikers into the street. He dropped the green blanket into a storefront. I stood powerless on the sidewalk, surrounded by the abandoned "I AM A MAN" placards, as the man leapt into his car and sped away.

His white Mustang vanished—disappeared into the bedlam of a world only beginning to comprehend that Dr. Martin Luther King had been shot dead on a motel balcony in the city of Memphis, Tennessee, in the early evening of Thursday, April 4, 1968.

CHAPTER EIGHTEEN

After the shooting, I stood alone on the sidewalk in a suspended silence, the kind like when you witness an accident about to happen and you cannot stop it, you can't shout quickly enough to interrupt it, and the moment before impact seems like an hour.

The quiet was quelled by the ringing of a bell, more furious than I had ever heard a bell rung. It was coming from the firehouse, and firemen struggled with their heavy jackets as they raced for their trucks.

All around me, screaming sirens came from every direction. I was surrounded by a swirling swarm of police vehicles. Officers emerged from their cruisers in flak jackets with their weapons raised; they moved in columns, pointing their guns in sharp, coordinated changes of direction. The rooming house was blocked by a line of patrolmen with gas masks and rifles pressed sideways against their chests.

I walked the short distance to the edge of the Lorraine Motel. Wails of anguish came from the shell-shocked members of Dr. King's camp.

"Where did the shot come from?" a police officer shouted.

Three people, kneeling next to Dr. King on the motel balcony, pointed in an upward direction toward the rooming house. King was prostrate in a pool of blood on the balcony concrete floor. A man held a white handkerchief to his forehead to stop the spurting stream.

Four policemen raced past me to the Lorraine. "I think I saw the shooter," I told one of them. "He came from the rooming house; he was wearing a dark suit and tie. He ran down the steps with what looked like a gun under a green blanket. He got into a white Mustang."

I listened as the policeman radioed what I had told him into his patrol car's intercom.

I had nowhere to go. Everyone around me had somewhere to be, a task to perform, and a family to comfort. I stood alone, alone on a sidewalk, and tried with no success to snatch still the spinning images in my head and make sense of them.

The Green Beetle was my only refuge. All around me, shopkeepers were boarding up and locking their stores. Shoppers with worried expressions loaded their packages into their cars and made their way through the maze of law enforcement in their paths.

When I got to the bar, it was closed tight, with a long metal brace locked over both the doors. The priest leaned up against the wall and cried when he saw me and tried to pull me down to sit next to him. He reeked of bourbon. I pulled away.

Ahead of me I could see the church steeple with its bell still askew from the morning's accident. My anxiety subsided when I remembered the full pint of vodka in my jacket pocket and thought perhaps I could sit inside the church a while.

When I reached the chapel, its huge wooden doors were locked tight. I sat there on the steps and felt inside my pocket for the pint. There was something else in that pocket, something I had not thought of in a while. It was the key, the key I kept with me always, the key to the box that held my writings, my mother's photographs, and everything I held dear.

On that church step, I ached for my mother in a way I never had before. I missed her so—the way she held me to her chest as I knelt next to her sickbed, and the way she smiled when I returned from the store with all the items from her list crossed off and then I put them away in her kitchen. It was her touch I missed most.

I thought of the man who lay bleeding on the Lorraine Motel balcony. He had millions of followers and a family that was now devastated, just as I had been with each loss I had suffered. But though I had just been a witness to a national tragedy, I could not think for long about Dr. Martin Luther King. I had another man on my mind. That man was Boaz Bartlett.

Hate is not always visible. It travels highways of its own; it finds crevices into places even the smallest rodent cannot squeeze; it feasts on us and then vomits us up to do its bidding. Hate replaced the very air in Memphis that day, and each one of us there sucked it into our lungs; no matter our race or religion or politics, we all hated someone that day. There was hate for the shooter, for the police, the strikers, the mayor, the blacks, and the whites. But me...I hated Boaz.

I downed the pint in a few swills and headed in the direction of Papa Jim's house and the truth, whatever is was, about my brother.

Under the awning of the Peabody Hotel, a group of people were gathered around a radio that spoke of Dr. King's transport to the hospital and his dire condition.

"Why did this have to happen in Memphis?" one man in the crowd lamented. News trucks went around police barricades, and reporters brushed past me on their way to the Lorraine.

I crossed Poplar Avenue in front of the police station, where just yesterday I had attended a meeting on how the city could avoid the catastrophe that had just occurred. Officers loaded their cruisers with heavy rounds of ammunition and muzzled German shepherds. The dogs jumped on their handlers, excited to be called into service. "Get in that car," an officer shouted, "we have to get this bastard."

Just off downtown I passed through the white neighborhoods of midtown. I saw worried men come home to locked doors as their families peered from behind closed curtains.

"I've taught you how to use this rifle; it will be by the front door. You use it to protect your mother and sister," I heard a man tell his son, who appeared to be about nine years old. The young boy nodded.

I walked through the black neighborhoods, where people wept together in the street. "They're gonna kill us all now, just you watch; we gotta fight back," a young man shouted from his front porch.

The sirens screamed from every direction. Authorities were not just searching for the shooter; they had a new problem: There was the smell of smoke coming from downtown, and the scarlet glow of fires reddened the twilight descending on Memphis. I could see Papa Jim's backyard just ahead of me.

I fell against the back wall of a clapboard house to catch my breath. Using the hunting pace of my brother, I made my way to the Bartlett fence with Indian-like, silent footsteps. From my position I could see Papa's back as he sat on the steps with his head held low in his hands.

Boaz wrapped his arm around his father, and there was the barrel of a shotgun resting across his lap. He had a weapon, and I needed one too. My brother might not be able to pull the trigger, but I could do what was necessary to protect myself.

I heard the television in the house as I crept into the old garage. I looked in the rubble for something I might use to defend myself.

From the television came the voice of Walter Cronkite: "Dr. Martin Luther King, the apostle of nonviolence in the civil-rights movement, has been shot dead in Memphis, Tennessee."

I heard Papa Jim cry out from an open window. Boaz took his father in his arms and rocked him side to side as the old man wept.

"Police have issued an all-points bulletin for a well-dressed, young white man seen running from the scene," Cronkite continued. "Dr. King was standing on a balcony of a second-floor hotel room when, according to a companion, a shot was fired from across the street. In the friend's words, the bullet exploded in his face. Dr. King has just been pronounced dead at a Memphis hospital."

I found a full can of gas next to the mower in the garage. The door to the Hippocrene Library was open. I picked up the gas can and went through the threshold. With no emotion, I poured the fuel over the books, the shelves, and the walls and floor.

I was not my brother, and I would not hesitate. I reached for the matches lying next to the stove, lit the gas, and walked out. I stepped back to watch it burn. For a moment there was a succulent silence, so I alone could watch the flames lick the building.

Even when the two men rushed from the house into the yard, I remained still. Boaz, Papa Jim, and I stared back at one another separated by the blaze. Then Boaz leapt into action to save the building, but it was already gone.

Papa Jim's gaze was transfixed on me. His dark skin glowed from the red reflection of the flames. His expression was the same as the face of my father the afternoon he wailed on our living room floor for my dead brother. I turned from his torture and walked down the street as if it were any ordinary Thursday.

When I got back to the rooming house, police were still swarming the block around the Lorraine Motel. An officer escorted me to Miss Bessie, who, even though distraught, confirmed I was a renter.

I needed a drink bad and rummaged through my belongings to locate my stash. There were two pints left in a drawer next to the Gideon Bible.

My hands shook so hard I had to hold the wrist of one to make the other steady. With the mattress replaced on my bed, I lay and listened to news reports that Memphis was under a strict dusk-to-dawn curfew, and all liquor stores would be closed until further notice. Cold sweat dampened my face and clothes.

I drank until I passed out with the Bible next to my pillow.

CHAPTER NINETEEN

The great city of Memphis—whose majestic bluffs Indian tribes had occupied for ten thousand years; whose ambitious founders named it for the ancient, glorious capital of Egypt; the place where Union naval forces wrested control from the Confederates; and the place where the yellow fever once wiped out 75 percent of its population—was suffering its saddest day.

The weight of despair was especially felt at City Hall, where, about an hour after the shooting, Mayor Henry Loeb sat behind his desk with his head held in his hands and listened over the police radio to the news.

No one thought to turn on the lights in his office, and with the dark paneling and the approaching twilight, he could hardly see the group of city councilmen gathered with him there. The only sound was the sobs of two black councilmen in the back of the room.

Loeb turned down the police radio, rose from the desk, and knelt next to the men. "I hope you know I never meant for any of this to happen. I'm just as sick about the loss of Dr. King as any of you."

Some of the councilmen exchanged glances and shook their heads. One grabbed his hat to leave, and as he walked out, he said, "Henry, this whole thing could have been avoided." He slammed the office door behind him.

Loeb clasped his hands and looked down at his desk as if in prayer, but really he was calculating his next move. "Get me the governor," he screamed to his secretary in the adjoining room.

"I want the National Guard brought back here immediately; this city is going under curfew. We are under lockdown until further notice," Loeb barked into the telephone.

Loeb hit the desk with his fist. "You fellas can believe what you want, but the truth is this garbage strike is an illegal labor dispute; now get out there and take care of your constituents."

When the room cleared, Loeb rose from his desk and locked his office door. There, where no would see or know, he laid his head on his desk and cried alone.

Bedlam descended on the Memphis police headquarters in the first hour after the shooting. The police director called in all available manpower.

"We need to find whoever did this and soon. These streets are gonna explode. Don't overreact," he said.

The director fully expected a night of mayhem. "I just hope the National Guard gets here, and quick," he told his officers.

In the beginning the authorities were surprised no rioting materialized. It was, as one officer said, "like when you burn your finger; it takes a couple of seconds for the pain to reach your brain." A few hours would pass before the rage detonated.

By nine o'clock there were reports of snipers and flames. Within an hour there were large fires in retail and industrial parts of the city. In the first hour of the curfew, both blacks and whites were in a panic to reach their homes. Many whites rushed home to load and ready their hunting rifles.

Blacks were suspicious that the Memphis police force had some responsibility for the assassination, though there was never any proof or credence given to their claims once the investigation was completed. The day before, Memphis had been like a vase filled with a bouquet of tolerance and trust for its citizens to enjoy, but today, that vase had been smashed into a thousand pieces on the balcony of the Lorraine Motel. Dr. King's brother and many of his associates remained at the motel, hoping their worst fears would not be realized. But when the devastating news finally arrived, the group moved to the home of Reverend Billy Kyles, where a large buffet that had been prepared for Dr. King was still on the dining-room table.

For two terrible nights, riots raged in large cities across the United States. In Memphis, a National Guard contingency of four thousand men was sent into the streets.

Later in the evening, a group of Dr. King's staff members returned to the balcony and, with a cardboard remnant, scraped his blood into a glass jar.

PART FOUR

Arriving Ragged and Torn

CHAPTER TWENTY

For the citizens of Memphis, Friday morning dawned with a feeling of dread. Schools and many businesses were closed, leaving people with idle time to worry about what would come next and from which direction. The news from the US Justice Department that the search for the killer had widened to hundreds of miles outside the city was a relief.

There was a good amount of physical evidence found in the first minutes after the assassination. The green bedspread with a gun wrapped inside had been dropped at a storefront not far from the rooming house. The killer was seen escaping in a white Mustang.

Many whites were unsure how to respond to the killing of Dr. King. As memorials and church services began to organize, there were sympathetic whites who felt their faces would not be welcome at black churches. Others reached out in spite of their trepidation, and most of their efforts were appreciated by the black community.

One notable event was a gathering of ministers, priests, and rabbis Friday morning in Mayor Loeb's office.

The mayor was polite but noncommittal. A rabbi appealed to Loeb by saying, "We must have laws. But I would remind you most respectfully, sir, that there are greater laws than the laws of Memphis and Tennessee...the laws of God. Let us not hide behind legal technicalities. Let us not wrap ourselves up in slogans. Let us do the will of God for the good of the city...that every person in this city can live with dignity and self-respect." Still, Loeb made no promises.

Prideful citizens became concerned about the legacy of shame the city would inherit from this heinous act by a killer who most likely was not one of them but who had forever scarred their reputations. When it was all over, the city had three civilian deaths, forty-seven serious injuries, 275 looted stores, and numerous fires.

By Friday afternoon forty cities were in major crisis from the assassination's backlash. Chicago, New York, Baltimore, and Pittsburgh were especially troubled with fires, rioting, and looting. Washington, DC, was a focal point, as smoke hung over the White House from over a hundred fires. President Johnson called in the regular army to supplement the efforts of the National Guard. Television viewers watched in horror as soldiers and paratroopers in combat fatigues could be seen trying to keep control in the nation's capital. When the toll was taken, 150 cities had fires and rioting. Forty people died, and several thousands suffered from injuries. Hard-hit Washington, DC, had property damages of more than $50 million.

In almost continuous session, the Memphis City Council busied itself with a resolution expressing sympathy and organizing reward monies for the killer's capture. They and local businessmen implored the mayor to settle the strike. By Saturday, lawyers and union officials were pouring into Memphis. Even President Johnson insisted on sending a representative; though warned by his lawyers that the federal government should not insert itself in local and state labor disputes, the president insisted.

When the president's envoy arrived at the Peabody Hotel, he saw the streets full of half-tracks and soldiers. The next morning, on the way to his first meeting with the mayor, the Washington mediator commented on how prosperous Memphis appeared, and that it did not seem like a place where such bitterness would reside. But when he arrived at City Hall, he was welcomed by layers and layers of armed guards toting rifles and pistols. After meeting with the mayor, surrounded by his guards, the man reported feeling like he was "in the midst of a Tennessee Williams play."

Mediating sessions among the various groups went on until after midnight Saturday. They reconvened on Sunday and worked through the night. For everyone at that table in the Claridge Hotel, it became apparent that optimism had no place in the room. With the world watching, both the city and union held their positions without exception.

One of the City Council's primary acts was to ensure the march that had been planned for Monday and that Dr. King had fought so hard to stage would go on as scheduled. Estimates of the number of possible marchers varied widely, but as the funeral for Dr. King would be held in Atlanta the day after the Memphis march, officials felt there would be thousands arriving from all parts of the country. They settled on what seemed a reasonable number of forty thousand marchers and continued to work night and day throughout the weekend to make certain the march was successful.

While lawyers, politicians, mediators, city planners, and ordinary citizens waded their way through the assassination's aftereffects, the garbage strikers continued their daily ritual on Main Street with "I AM A MAN" placards.

On a gray, cloud-laden day, Monday, April 8, the promise of a peaceful march would be kept to the late Dr. King. The city's estimates were right; there were national news reports of from thirty-five thousand to forty-two thousand in attendance. The march moved from the streets of Hernando to Linden, Linden to Main, and on to City Hall. They were escorted by police, five thousand National Guardsmen, photographers, cameramen, helicopters, M48 tanks, and reporters. Very few spectators watched from the streets, where store windows were boarded up. In contrast, floral funeral wreaths hung on some of the businesses' locked doors.

At the intersection of Main and Beale, Mrs. King and three of her children joined the marchers. From throughout the United States, politicians, movie stars, religious leaders, and union officials held hands with the marchers. The Memphis police commissioner stayed close to Mrs. King. Her safety in his city was paramount in his mind that day.

Though the majority of marchers were black, there were smatterings of white locals in the crowd. One Episcopal priest summed up the feelings for all sides when he admitted to retrieving his last will and testament as he departed for the march and leaving it with his secretary in case it was needed.

The next day in Atlanta, one hundred thousand people marched behind a mule-drawn caisson in the funeral precession. Among them were several Memphis City Council members. Dr. Martin Luther King was finally at rest, but Memphis was just awakening to his passing and its repercussions.

Negotiations at the Claridge Hotel to end the strike continued through all this. The atmosphere became so charged that Loeb and the union representative were separated and only brought together when necessary.

Every city official knew there was going to be a settlement, and one expressed his goal by saying, "We didn't feel like we could capitulate and give them carte blanche to the rape of the city, which is what is wanted."

Many in the room felt the opposing parties would just walk out. But somehow, a settlement began to emerge. Most of the demands were easily resolved, but the sticking points returned to union recognition and the dues checkoff. Legal wrangling finally worked through these barriers too. In the end, the city had no money in the budget to fund the raises for the remainder of the year. The impasse was ended by a Jewish executive, who in 1908, at the age of sixteen, had borrowed $125 from his father to fund a business selling homemade potions from a horse and wagon in Memphis and the countryside. His company had become one of the country's greatest success stories, with consumer products in every grocery and drug store in America. Long known for his benevolence, Abe Plough saw a way to stop the misery and gave the city $60,000 to fund the raises.

In the sixty-fifth day after the strike started, the union meeting became a place of joy and laughter. The garbagemen had won their own private war, a war that demanded the world be halted on its axis and take notice of their lonely crusade.

As one union official put it: "'I am a man!' They meant it. They wanted, even though they were the men who picked up the garbage and threw it into trucks, they wanted somebody for the first time to say, 'You are a man!' It was the real thing."

CHAPTER TWENTY-ONE

On my lumpy mattress in the rooming house, I dreamed of the Chandler farm. It was an early-spring afternoon as I drove the tractor out of the shop; anything seemed possible. I was so happy. My father had kept his promise and stayed sober for eight months now. My mother was busy with dinner in the kitchen, fully recovered from cancer surgery. My brother banged the back door as he came home from football practice and announced, "I'm starving."

From above, a chair raked across the floor, and I woke to my living nightmare. The mattress below me was damp from my profuse sweat, which now had settled on my hands and forehead. I trembled so hard my body rocked.

I needed a drink so bad I would have sacrificed breathing for it. Then I remembered there was nothing left to drink, and no place open to get one. The reflex to vomit was the only motivation I had to rise from bed.

After I cleaned the vomit from my face, the room felt claustrophobic, and I wobbled to the stairs and held onto the rail. When I reached the street, hundreds of people milled around, asking one another questions that had no answers.

In a nearby diner, I ordered coffee and eggs. I knew that I had been drinking for a while but couldn't remember how long. Hot coffee did nothing to quell my internal trembling. I was sick and needed help. I pushed my plate away and decided Papa Jim's house was the best place for me to recover.

Squinting, I checked the angle of the sun and calculated it must be late morning as I walked down blocks of burned buildings and streets filled with broken glass.

Confused, I trekked through the business district and crossed into the threshold of neighborhoods. The fronts of the homes were crowded with people, but the atmosphere was not jovial. Many were just standing around, looking off into space. A few talked low among themselves. People stared at me.

I needed to vomit and found a storm drain on the street, and my breakfast burned as it heaved into my throat and spewed into the street. A mother shielded her children and rushed them into the house to keep them from being infected by my presence.

Two hours passed while I alternately vomited and stumbled. I was so weak that my confusion turned to panic.

Papa Jim's house was on a slight rise. He and Boaz were on the front porch surrounded by neighbors. I called out to them, and it was the image of their bewildered faces that was the last thing I recall before losing consciousness.

It took four people to drag me into the house. Papa Jim wiped my face with an ice-filled towel and forced so much water into me that I screamed, "Stop!"

From the kitchen window, I saw Boaz get into his car, slam the door, and screech out of the driveway in a hurry. The neighbors lifted me into the bedroom and laid me onto the bed, which was covered with my sweat in mere moments.

"I need a drink, Papa. *Please*, I need a drink."

Papa Jim slammed me back onto the bed. "Your drinking days are over, Cotton. You're lucky to be alive," he said. "There is no alcohol in this house, and someone is going to sit right here with you until the DTs pass. Now get to sleep; you have worn my nerves to a nub."

It was Friday, April 5. I slept the rest of that day and most of the next. Papa Jim brought me clear soup and water every few hours. I was too weak to resist his efforts.

CHAPTER TWENTY-TWO

Sunday was what we used to call a lead day: gray and rainy. My sleepy eyes rested on the back of Boaz as he sat reading the *Commercial Appeal* newspaper at the kitchen table. I could smell coffee and bacon, and I was really hungry for the first time in weeks.

My stirring signaled Boaz to turn and face me. "Where's Papa Jim?" I asked.

"He's gone to the Memphis Cares rally at Crump Stadium," Boaz answered.

The newspapers on the kitchen table bellowed the bold headline, "KING DEATH WILL NOT DETER PEACE MARCH: MRS. KING AND FAMILY WILL ATTEND."

The words of those headlines stuffed me into an envelope, stamped and dated April 7, 1968, and delivered me into reality. The realization of Boaz's shocking confession prior to the assassination raced through me again. There he sat, casually eating breakfast and ignoring me. I pulled the back of his chair hard so that it tipped over backward, and he was barely able to recover enough to stand.

"What the hell, Cotton?"

"*Did. You. Kill. My. Brother?*" I screamed. "You killed my brother because he couldn't get a shot off?"

"Calm down, Cotton; let me tell you what happened," he said.

"You want to kill me, too? Is that what you want? That man in the Outrigger Bar...was he supposed to kill me?" I said.

I became an animal, a physical beast whose juices craved blood and meat. I became an energy so profound that it could only be satiated by the butchering of Boaz. My tiger body sprang from the ground, and I roared as I tackled him and knocked him from the chair. We wrestled on the floor, Boaz at a disadvantage because of his still weak and bandaged arm.

A bellow from the parlor room thundered, "*Silence!*" When Papa Jim took a giant step into the kitchen, he was still holding the Memphis Cares program in his hand. He slammed it down onto the table and drew both of us by the collar and heaved us into the kitchen chairs.

When my chair stopped rocking on its legs, I could see the view from the window for the first time. It was then that I remembered the library in the yard and what I had done.

Profound pain poured over me. Even for a man who was no stranger to suffering, it had the power to overwhelm. "*What...have...I...done?*"

I had set fire to the Hippocrene Library. My body crumpled to the ground. I lay in a fetal position and moaned, rocked in agony. I grabbed Papa Jim's ankles with both hands. "Please forgive me, Papa; please forgive me."

Over and over I wept and wailed for Papa Jim's forgiveness. He looked down at me and, with an unsympathetic jerk, raised me with both his hands to standing and threw me against the stove.

"Quit the sniveling. You have done what you have done. Now you are gonna have to live with it."

Through clenched teeth Papa Jim looked from me to Boaz. "Sit down, both of you. What's goin' on between the two of you?"

"He knew my brother in Vietnam. I think he killed him," I said.

Papa Jim's head jerked to face Boaz. "Is that true?"

"I knew him; I didn't kill him...but I watched him die."

"Boaz, you tell us right now what happened. All of it."

Boaz took a deep breath and began to talk: "That first night when Cotton came to stay with us and he told us about his family, I couldn't believe it, but I knew they were both from Marianna because his brother talked all the time about what a Podunk place it was. I'd heard so much of it before. I knew they had to be brothers."

"Why didn't you tell Cotton that night...or later?" Papa asked.

"Because I could see he'd lost his whole family. He didn't need any more heaped on him."

"Well, that's noble, Boaz, but I get the feelin' there's a lot you're not tellin' us," Papa Jim said.

"I had three men with me, and Cotton's brother had his three. We went into an abandoned encampment. They got there first, and Cotton's brother...he sent his men to look in the tents so, y'know—to see if there were any supplies in there."

"How far back were you and your men?" Papa asked.

"Not far; one of my men sighted a sniper in a tree through his binoculars. He yelled out to warn your brother."

"Go on," I said.

"Your brother saw the sniper and raised his gun. He just looked at him; he panicked and never fired a shot. His men were sitting ducks."

I laid my head on the table, overcome with the nausea and the memory of my brother, the deer that got away, and the football never thrown.

"Your brother ran off. My men followed him while I helped took care of the dead."

"Then what?" Papa Jim prodded him to continue.

"I heard a shot and ran a half-mile and found my men standing over your brother. We tried to save him, but he was already dead."

"What do you mean you couldn't do somethin' to keep them from killing my brother? That's cold-blooded murder. Why didn't you turn them in?"

"I did. One of the men confessed and hung himself in his prison cell two days later. He had a wife and eight-year-old twin boys."

The three of us sat in silence for several minutes. I looked out at the destruction of the library and shook my head.

Finally, Papa Jim said, "There's more, isn't there, Boaz?"

"Yes, sir," Boaz said.

"Are you ready to hear this, Cotton?" Papa turned to me.

"I want to know everything," I said.

"We all hated your brother," Boaz continued. "He stole food and boots and rifles and sold them to the Viet Cong."

I put my head in my hands and tried to stop it from spinning. I felt sick.

"He stole some poor sap's girlfriend. The kid showed all of us her picture, and your brother somehow managed to get her address. He started writing to her...told her he'd fallen in love with her just from seeing her picture."

"So?" I said.

"She broke it off with the guy, told him she was in love with your brother. He laughed about it until...until the guy killed himself. I have her parents' phone number if you don't believe me.

"One of his favorite stories was about how he used to steal liquor to make sure your dad was drunk before his football games. He said it got him sympathy from his teachers and was the best way to pick up women."

"That's enough," I said.

Papa Jim moved his chair next to mine and cradled my head against his chest. "This is tough, son. I know it is."

Boaz rose from his chair and went into his bedroom. When he came back, he laid something in front of me. It was my brother's dog tag and a photograph of him in a group of soldiers with Boaz. They were all laughing together.

"There's just one more thing, Boaz. What have I done to *you?* You almost got me killed in that bar," I said.

"I don't know, Cotton. I wish I did know why I did that. Your mannerisms, the way you talk. I just can't stand the sight of you."

"Is that everything?" Papa asked.

"It's most of it," said Boaz.

Papa Jim rose and began to stir in the kitchen. Boaz and I sat there with our own thoughts. In a few minutes, the smell of brewing coffee filled the room.

Papa Jim poured cups for all of us and sat down. "I've made a decision. Here's what we're gonna do, boys." I looked down at the table where Papa had placed the Memphis Cares flyer. There was a drawing of Dr. King on the front, and the words read, "Memphis Cares: A Bi-Racial Rally of Healing for the City of Memphis."

"Boaz is shipping out in four days," he said.

"You know, Cotton," Boaz interrupted his father, "what you did to my father and the library, it wasn't right."

My face flamed from embarrassment and shame. "If you'd told me the truth in the beginning, none of this would have ever happened."

"Silence!" Papa slammed his hand down on the kitchen table. "Both of you have lost the right to speak in my presence."

Boaz and I were both so startled that neither one of us argued.

"I told you I've made a decision, and I mean it. I want the two of you to spend the next three days cleaning up the mess from the fire and getting the yard prettied up. I have a photographer coming in a few days to take family pictures. There are to be *no* words between you...total silence for three days. You both need to think about what you've done."

Boaz and I nodded as we agreed to Papa Jim's decision.

"When the Hippocrene has been laid to rest, Cotton, you can help me get Boaz ready to ship out," he said.

I nodded to Papa Jim.

He looked at me deep in the eye, just as he had the first time I had met him. "Starting tonight, you'll stay here with me a while. I want to be the first person you see every morning, and I want mine to be the last face you see at night. You're gonna look at that burned building every single day."

"Okay," I said in a whisper.

"Boaz, you take this photograph of Cotton's brother, and you keep it in your breast pocket. I expect you to look at it every day, every single day."

"Yes, sir," Boaz said and put the photograph in his shirt pocket.

"You take the picture back to the war with you. You think about hate, you think about it until you don't have any of it left in your heart. Then you bring that picture back to Cotton when you have forgiven him."

"Cotton, you need to go get your things at the rooming house. You're gonna stay here with me for a few months. If you run now, you'll always just be somebody's little brother. You got to learn to be your own man."

I nodded.

"Now, go on; you need to find some kinda job starting next week, but first we're gonna get this mess cleaned up."

Once on the street, I headed for the rooming house, and I worked out a plan. I found a telephone booth and called Froggie and told him I had business in Memphis and would not be home for a while. I then called Mr. Chandler and told him the same, and not to expect me before the harvest, if even then. It must have been the tone in my voice. Neither one of them questioned me.

When I got to the rooming house, Miss Bessie was there. She still looked pale and broken. I told her I was moving out today, but that I needed a job. I thought maybe she could use some rest and I could help out at the rooming house. The relief that came over her face was her answer.

We agreed on an hourly wage, and I told her I would start next week. She would take an extended vacation and visit her sister in Florida.

Papa Jim sat on the porch and looked across the yard at the remnants of the Hippocrene when I came back to the house, with my meager belongings in a small cardboard box.

"Papa," I said in a soft voice, "I've gotta job at the rooming house." When he turned to look at me, I could see that he had been crying, probably for some time. He rose from the chair, went into his bedroom, and closed the door. He went to sleep that night with no dinner, but he left two plates on the table for me and Boaz. They were still warm, covered in aluminum foil.

I ate my dinner alone and went to my room to unpack. It was still twilight, and from my bedroom window, I noticed a young boy from the neighborhood coming down the sidewalk on his bike. When he saw the burned building, he dropped his bike and walked into the yard to survey the damage.

He was about eight or nine and had thick, black glasses that he kept pushing back on his nose. He picked up some of the ashes and let the wind blow them from his hand. He stood there a long while before getting back on his bike and making his way through the neighborhood.

I went about unpacking my clothes; most of the things in the box had been bought for me by the FBI. Once finished, I went into the bathroom and took the top flap from the box and cut a piece to fit over the upper portion of the mirror. I cut it so it would fit just right between the mirror and its silver frame. It worked fine. I could use that in the mornings to shave and take it down so that Boaz and Papa could use the full mirror.

When I came back into my room, Boaz had been there. He had left a note resting on the pillow. It read, "If you want the military to do a full investigation of your brother's death, you can contact the following." A name and phone number were written on it. I took the note and put it at the bottom of my sock drawer, and slammed the drawer shut.

I had been unable to write in my journal for a long time, but I kept it with me and sometimes slept with it next to me. Something in that handwritten note made me pick it up and begin to write. Just feeling the journal in my hand and picking up a pen to write made my stomach flop.

CHAPTER TWENTY-THREE

When I woke, the only noise in the house was the drone of the television running a series of special reports on the assassination, the riots, the upcoming march, and the hunt for the killer. It was the first day of the silence.

Papa Jim left for his job at the Peabody before I woke. Boaz and I ate our breakfast with no words between us, as directed. Without it being said, we both knew there'd better be significant progress made on the cleaning before Papa got home that evening.

While Boaz cleaned the kitchen, I retrieved the tools from the garage. The shovel, wheelbarrows, and rakes were still in the same place where I had seen them last Thursday night, as well as the gas can I had used to burn the building. I brought the tools to Boaz. He wouldn't look at me.

When I was mute for those months earlier in my life, I understood it was a time of grace to heal, but this silence was a punishment. There were words bubbling to the surface, angry hate-filled words that I stuffed back down my throat. Boaz and I attacked the ashes and burned out walls with our backs to one another.

Within minutes sweat dripped from both of our chins, and when I looked over at Boaz, his jaw was clenched. The only thing that kept us from breaking into a fistfight was the fear of the old man at the Peabody.

By midmorning we had been so physically active, our aching muscles and fatigue dampened our rage. I even managed a smirk when I saw Boaz rub his mangled arm.

Boaz took his lunch break on the front porch steps while I ate my sandwich in the kitchen. I finished first and took a load of ashes in the wheelbarrow and dumped them into a ravine in the backyard.

As I came around from the back of the house, a neighbor stood in the middle of the charred remains of the library. With him was a man in a suit with a camera and a notebook. The man took photographs of the blackened pile as the neighbor described what the building once looked like.

The neighbor pointed to Boaz and asked if Mr. Bartlett could be found at the Peabody this afternoon. Boaz nodded. Curiosity overrode our anger for a brief moment as we shrugged our shoulders at one another. We went back to work until dinner, ate in the silence, and went to bed early.

Day two, the silence. When I got to breakfast, Boaz was already drinking his last cup of coffee and handed me the *Commercial Appeal* newspaper that Papa left on the table with a note attached to read an article at the bottom of page two.

Memphis, Tennessee, April 8, 1968—Thursday's assassination of Dr. Martin Luther King was a day of double tragedy for Mr. James Bartholomew Bartlett, who is a long-time employee of the Peabody Hotel. A Negro, Mr. Bartlett is a self-educated man who describes himself as a polyhistor. The word "polyhistor" comes from the Greek language and means a learned man.

He began collecting books while a navy sailor and used his spare time to visit the libraries and local landmarks of the countries where he was stationed throughout his 20-year military service.

When Mr. Bartlett returned to Memphis, his wife and young son often joined him on his searches for discarded books. He also worked odd jobs for money to buy the great literature of the world, eventually building a library of a several hundred volumes. Mr. Bartlett called it the Hippocrene Library for the mythological fountain on Mt. Helicon. The Greeks believed the fountain was a sacred source of inspiration for the muses and was formed by the hoof of winged horse Pegasus.

During the riots of April 4, the Hippocrene Library was destroyed by fire. Yesterday he was quoted as saying, "The fire cannot burn the thirst in my heart for knowledge. It did not destroy the education I have from my years of study. One day I will be laid to rest a learned man, with or without the library." Mr. Bartlett has no plans to rebuild.

Boaz and I picked up the tools and returned to work. I hadn't slept well. I kept waking from a dream that the police were looking for me. The newspaper assumed the fire was set in response to the riots. Papa Jim could have had me arrested, and I spent the afternoon of silence pondering why he hadn't when he had every right.

We made progress, but the ashes were now damp from dew, and a crust had formed over them, which made it harder to break them up the deeper we shoveled. Boaz's arm hurt. It had healed on the outside, but he had lost significant strength to atrophy.

I stared at him as he worked, daring him to stop. It became a game. He tried to sneak in a few moments' rest, and I kept my eyes on him to mock his defeats. The silence wore on; the day was long, made longer by the interminable quiet.

Unknown to us that morning, the wife of a prominent attorney lingered over the Hippocrene news article. Once her children were dropped off at their private school, she made phone calls to her garden club and church friends, who responded to her conversation with mixed reactions, ranging from polite coolness to outright hostility. She was able, however, to persuade three of them to support a cause.

Over dinner that evening her husband was incredulous. "What did you say?"

"I simply asked my friends if they had read the newspaper account of Mr. Bartlett's loss and inquired if they could help me collect books to encourage him to rebuild the library. I told them it was a small step in rebuilding relations with the negroes. I don't understand why you had calls from their husbands today. I don't think it's an unreasonable request, and I expect your support."

With resignation in his voice, her husband said, "All right, after dinner I'll see what I can spare in my office."

"Thank you," she replied.

"But you listen to me, I forbid you from going into that part of town alone. I'll give the yardman some extra money

Saturday to get you there and back safely. Don't argue with me about it."

"Yes, dear, I understand."

"I don't want to be on the golf course and have to come rescue you from this adventure. You mind your step."

We completed the cleanup by late afternoon. Where once the Hippocrene Library stood, there was now a black spot on the ground, with ashes piled in a ravine. When Papa arrived home from work, he pronounced the job finished.

"All right, boys, that looks fine. Now tomorrow I want this yard put in pristine shape."

Boaz and I both leaned on our rakes and nodded.

"I have a friend coming over in the afternoon to take pictures before Boaz leaves, and I want it perfect."

Day three of the silence. It was Saturday morning. Boaz and I cleaned the yard as Papa Jim supervised from the porch.

"Cotton, you trimmed the shrubs all crooked; now get back over there."

I was the first to notice the crowd of neighbors forming in the middle of the street. There were enough people that cars had to snake around the throng coming in our direction. Some neighbors walked backward, while others formed a phalanx around something we couldn't see.

Papa Jim and Boaz joined me to stare at the street and the curiosity coming our way. Then we saw them. A thin, elderly black man was struggling under the weight of a large carton. He wore baggy pants tied up with a rope for his belt. He had worked for the lawyer's wife for twenty-two years. Behind him were four white ladies, all holding books in both hands. They wore scarves on their heads, pearls under their neat dress collars, and low heels.

"Well, I never," said Papa Jim.

The crowd stopped and gathered around the women on the sidewalk. One of the ladies called out, "Are you Mr. James Bartholomew Bartlett?"

Papa Jim answered, "I am, ma'am, and I am pleased to have you ladies at my home. What can I do for you?"

"We represent a contingent of Christian women in the city of Memphis who want to encourage you to rebuild the library. We've brought three dozen volumes to help you get a good start," she replied.

"That's very kind of you, and I'll take it under consideration," Papa answered.

The yardman lifted the carton to Papa Jim, but Papa didn't take it from him right away. He gave a long deep stare into the man's eyes, just as he had with me the first time I met him. But this man, this man who tended the yards of the powerful looked right back into Papa's eyes and into their knowing together.

The women departed as they came with a crowd of onlookers as escorts. I saw a young boy in the swarm. It was the same boy with the glasses I had seen from my bedroom window a few nights before. Now, with a closer look, I could see the child had the habit of pushing his glasses back on his nose because they were held together on one of the spring arms with a Band-Aid.

When we washed up after work, the smell of spaghetti wafted through the house. Papa Jim had prepared a feast of Boaz's favorite dishes. There was lemon-icebox pie piled high with whipped cream for dessert.

Papa had splurged and bought a nice bottle of wine. I was served iced tea. With the light of the candles on the table, the room seemed softer, and Papa's voice trembled as he prayed, "Dear Lord, we need your mighty sword of protection over the head of my son as he enters battle once again. May you bless those of us around this table and may these two young men reunite with peace in their hearts one day."

We ate our dinner in silence. *The Lawrence Welk Show* played from the parlor television set. After dinner I cleaned the kitchen to give Papa Jim time alone with Boaz.

When I brought their pie, Papa Jim spoke with Boaz as all men do when their sons go off to war.

"Son, just come back to me; don't let them take you away from me. I've lost your mother; I can't lose you."

We watched the dancers sweep across the television screen as we ate dessert. Papa put down his plate and looked from me to Boaz. "Do you two believe in coincidences? Seems odd to me the way you met in Memphis and the truth between you two came out just at the moment the gun was fired at Dr. King. You might think about that. Do you ever think about what the man who died right there in front of you would do? Seems to me Dr. King was forgiving and that you might have been there for a reason."

Boaz and I looked at one another, and even in the silence we both knew this was the first time either one of us had considered what Papa just said as a possibility.

"Kinda strange, isn't it?" Papa said.

I had promised Miss Bessie to run by after dinner for last-minute instructions before her trip to Florida, so I left through the back door after I washed the dessert plates.

As I traversed the same neighborhood yards as the night I had set the Hippocrene on fire, Papa's words played in my head. Was the bus ride I made across the Mississippi River that tossed me into a drink of death and confusion part of some grand universal game plan?

I didn't get far before I realized I was so consumed by my thoughts that I had made a wrong turn. I was lost.

I looked around to get my bearings. I was at Front and Jefferson in front of a twelve-story building I hadn't before noticed. Down the side of the building was a lighted sign, sparkling in the twilight. It read, Hotel King Cotton, Est. 1925. The irony of seeing my name paired with Dr. King's raised the hair on my neck.

CHAPTER TWENTY-FOUR

It was Sunday morning, the day of the departure. Boaz looked impressive in his uniform. Papa declared the end of the silence at breakfast, but we still didn't talk to one another much.

Neighbors gathered in the front yard to see Boaz in his dress military and to wish him well. I stood alone on the sidewalk while photographs were taken of Boaz and Papa Jim. Papa had his arm around his son's shoulders, and Boaz leaned into his dad. They both had broad smiles.

A friend loaded us into his old Ford for the trip to the bus station. Papa Jim rubbed Boaz's mangled arm all the way to the station. There were more than a hundred uniformed men hugging their tearful children and wives in the lobby.

Papa Jim held Boaz for a long time. "Boaz, you got the picture of Cotton's brother with you?"

"Yes, sir. Yes, sir, I do."

Papa cried as he said to us, "I want the two of you to shake hands."

Boaz and I refused to look one another in the eye but had a quick handshake. A buddy walked over and introduced himself and motioned for Boaz to come sit with him on the bus. Boaz took his father and lifted him from the ground with a long bear hug. He turned to join his friend, and then he was gone.

Papa Jim needed help to walk. He was so weak I felt his strength just give way under my grasp. "Come on now, I'll take you to the car."

When we reached the curb, the bus pulled away from the station. Other family members were waving good-bye to their loved ones. Papa dropped to the ground with his head in his hands. "I'm never going to see my Boaz again, Cotton."

"Come on now, you're just upset. Let's go home," I said. He nodded. "You know, Papa, I could rebuild the library. I've got some money saved; I could use it to buy the lumber."

The thought pushed Papa to regain himself. "No, Cotton, I'm not gonna make it that easy for you."

Papa went to bed for the rest of the day when we got home, and I had the house to myself. I spent the time drawing library plans and sketches in my journal.

On Monday morning we took the bus to work together, and the ordinary act was a relief. For the first since I had known her, Miss Bessie took down her curlers to reveal soft gray hair in waves around her smiling face as she handed me the keys to the rooming house and went over the accounting details one last time.

After dinner in the evening, the telephone rang as we were having ice cream on the porch. Boaz had promised his father he would call before he left the country, and I felt sure this must be from him.

Once Papa Jim hung up the phone and came outside, he stood on the porch, looking at the street for a long while. I finally asked, "Is everything okay with Boaz?"

"Yes, he's fine. He said that long-haired hippies threw eggs at them and called them baby killers in the airport. California is a strange place."

"Must be," I said.

"Cotton, he told me something else that's curious. He said while he was waiting for his flight, he picked up a copy of the *San Francisco Chronicle*, and there was an article about the Hippocrene fire in it."

"What? How could that have happened?" I asked.

"Why would anyone care about an old negro man's shack of books?" Papa asked and went to his bedroom to think about it.

CHAPTER TWENTY-FIVE

*T*hough he did not know it until much later, the man in the white Mustang was assisted in his escape from Memphis by a prank report of a high-speed chase through the busy streets. The precious minutes wasted for the police to determine the call was a hoax allowed the man to make his way into Mississippi and head south. He would drive through the night to Birmingham, and he made the risky decision to go to Atlanta to pick up a few personal belongings.

His arrogance was appalling. He returned to Dr. King's hometown, the city where King's new widow was trying to comfort her children following the news of his death. As he listened to radio reports of the assassination, he became convinced he was the most-wanted man in America. He knew he would have to abandon the Mustang and rethink his plan to drive it to Mexico.

At the Atlanta Greyhound bus station, he bought a ticket for Cincinnati, and later that night he took another bus bound for Detroit. He arrived there the morning of April 6 to a city that had *dealt with riots, looting, and arson since the killing. Now the streets were filled with three thousand National Guardsmen.*

He decided Canada was his best option. Though he knew the border crossing required no documentation, he still felt anxious he would arouse suspicion. He left the terminal to find a barber for a shave and haircut, as he thought his three-day-old beard might draw attention from the border guards. He knew that, even though the security at the crossing between the United States and Canada was normally lax, his crime would certainly make all movement out of the country more complicated. He need not have worried. Back at the bus terminal, he grabbed a cab to a train station and took the four-hour rail trip to Toronto.

After renting a room, he settled in for the weekend to watch the news reports on television. He learned of the riots in major cities and that Washington was especially troubled. He found out that the Academy Awards, the National Hockey League playoff game in St. Louis, and the season openers of seven Major League Baseball teams had all been rescheduled.

April 7 was Palm Sunday. He read in the newspaper that ten thousand people, both black and white, had gathered at Crump Stadium for an event called Memphis Cares. The Canadian woman who had rented the man the room noticed his odd behavior and worried brow. At dinner that evening, she asked her husband, "Do you think it's possible someone could escape from that mental hospital in town? We had a strange fella check in today."

On Monday morning he visited a Toronto library and researched microfilm for birth announcements from the 1930s. There he found a name to his liking and decided this would be his new identity. As he listened to the funeral and procession for Dr. King in Atlanta, he composed a letter to the registrar of births to change his name and mailed it later in the day.

A few days later, he would purchase a makeup kit from a Toronto theatrical supply company. He parted his hair in a different way and applied the makeup, along with a new pair of dark, horn-rimmed glasses. He donned his usual suit, and after looking in the mirror, he was satisfied with his new appearance. On April 11, he went into a photography studio and had a passport photo taken for his borrowed identity.

CHAPTER TWENTY-SIX

The Saturday after Boaz left, we finished supper and Papa rocked back in his chair and said, "You know, you seem to have some time after work, and you probably could help me out a little around here if you don't mind."

I responded with a thumbs-up, and Papa handed me a list. It was a long list:

- Mildew around the crawl spaces.
- New roof.
- Six lights need electrical work.
- Loose boards on the front and back porches.
- Four stuck windows.
- Clean and repair garage.
- Paint house.

I shook my head and laughed. "Did you leave anything out? Are you sure this is all?"

Boaz's treasured Chevy needed protection, so we decided to start with the garage.

By noon I had made progress. The trash bin behind the house was filled to overflowing, and I stacked several loads next to it and thought of the garbagemen marching in the streets with their signs; they would be the same men who would come to pick up the remains of the mess I had made of my life.

"Papa, could you find me a lantern, so I can finish this up after supper...Papa?" He had not heard. In fact, he had been distracted all day. He had not spoken a word to me the entire afternoon.

All day he had puttered around the house, never even coming out to the garage to check my progress.

I followed him into the house to locate a lantern and he said, "Before you go back to work, I've got something to show you."

He brought to the table a box, which he said had arrived the day before. Papa took the contents and laid them on the table between us.

Inside were three books about James Cook, the renowned British explorer, the first European to navigate Australia, New Zealand, and Hawaii. There was also a book about the botanist Joseph Banks, who traveled with Cook to Australia and became a British luminary for his findings.

"Who sent these to you?" I asked.

"Cotton, I don't know how this coulda happened. There's a note here from a professor with the Massachusetts Institute of Technology."

"What's it say?"

"It says he read about the Hippocrene in the *New York Times,* and these books are three of his favorites. He thought I might enjoy them too."

It took a moment for this to soak in, and I finally said, "I've never seen the *New York Times.* Where's Massachusetts, Papa?"

"Let me get the map. I'll show you."

Papa retrieved a huge map from a closet, the kind tacked to the bulletin board of every fifth-grade classroom. He pointed up north to Massachusetts. We looked at each other for a long time, both of us struggling to understand how this had happened.

"Papa, how did he know your address?" I asked.

"That's strange too. Look at this," he said. Papa showed me the top of the carton, and the address simply read, "Hippocrene Library, Memphis, Tennessee."

Papa held each book next to his face, so he could feel and smell the leather binding. He slowly flipped through the pages and read the table of contents of all three of them. From the window in the garage, I could see he had fallen to sleep in the rocking chair with the books in his lap. Just a couple of more loads of trash, and I would be finished.

My brother had taught me to be like the Indians: to keep my eyes and ears open to everything around me and never be taken by surprise. But late on a Saturday night, after more than twelve hours of hard work, my guard was down, so when the six men carrying torches and clubs stood outside the garage as I brought out the last load, I was more than surprised; I was frightened.

The leader spoke in a soft, seething voice through his teeth. "Boaz told us you burned down the library. Why you wanna do that, white boy? We knew you were trouble when you showed up in this neighborhood."

I dropped the box and held my hands above my head and said, "I don't want any trouble."

Unconvinced, the largest of the group threw me against the building. He cupped my head in his hands and slammed it against the garage three times.

"Get your honky ass out of here, do you understand?"

The back of my head was bleeding, and I was too dazed to respond. The next blows came to my stomach.

From the shadows came a booming voice, backed up by a shotgun's blast.

"Boys, you must have misunderstood Boaz. This man here is gonna help me rebuild the library. Appreciate your concern, but you go on back home now, and don't come back. I mean it now."

CHAPTER TWENTY-SEVEN

I spent the next day lying around the house, nursing my wounds. Papa took over all the chores and brought my meals to the couch.

"Do you really want to rebuild the library like you said last night?" I called after him as he took my plate to the kitchen.

He washed the dishes at the sink and acted as though he had not heard me. "What about it, you want me to draw up some plans?"

Still no answer, but I watched him as he puttered about the house and stacked and restacked books in the carton brought by the ladies. He turned the volumes over and over in his hands, looked through the pages, and took the time to read passages from many of them.

We settled into a routine of work and home life as I spent all my spare time working on the home repairs. In the evenings I wrote in my journal.

On a late Tuesday afternoon, Papa and I, both tired from a long day at work, rounded the corner for the short walk to the house from the bus stop. We could see a group of neighbors waiting in the front yard. Papa stopped dead in his tracks. We both feared the worst, that it would be news from Vietnam.

My heart beat fast as I ran ahead. I wanted to get there first to soften the blow of whatever was coming. When I reached the yard, the neighbors were talking and laughing. They pointed to the front porch. I waved my arm in the air to motion Papa to hurry.

There on the stoop were fifteen boxes and more than twenty-five letters. We looked at one another in disbelief.

"What do you think all this is?" he asked.

I shrugged my shoulders.

I brought Papa a knife from the kitchen, and he opened the boxes. They were all filled with books. One was even postmarked from Italy.

Papa shook his head and said, "I just don't understand what is happening here."

Over the next weeks, the boxes and letters swelled to such a substantial surge that coming home from work became an adventure. The neighbors were just as excited as Papa about the world coming to their door. Groups of them waited for us when we walked from the bus stop.

Papa read off the postmarks from the porch steps: "Biloxi, Mississippi; Toronto, Canada; San Jose, California; Toulon, France; Detroit, Michigan." And so it went for weeks.

One Saturday when I came down from working on the roof, Papa had the map of the world on the dining room wall; he had placed pins on all the distant places that found their way to his front porch.

"You're gonna need more pins for that map," I said.

"I know; I'll pick some up Monday. I thought the neighbors would like to see where all these books are coming from."

His high spirits gave me the courage to once again bring up the idea of rebuilding. "You're gonna need a place to keep all those books, Papa."

He didn't answer at first but went into his bedroom and brought back a cigar box. "I think you're right," he said, his eyes shining with tears.

Inside the box were dozens of letters, and many had money inside. When we went through and counted the donations, they amounted to over $5,000.

"I've never seen this much money, Papa."

"Me neither; it scares me to look at it."

"What do you wanna do with it?"

"Well, I've been lyin' awake at night thinkin' about that, and I owe three thousand dollars on this house. If I pay that off, Boaz will never have to worry about a place to live."

"That makes sense. What about the rest?"

"Let's rebuild the library, and this time let's do it for the neighborhood," he said.

We sat there a long time, each with our own thoughts. Finally, Papa said, "Cotton, I still can't get my head around how this happened."

"Me neither, Papa, me neither."

On his old Olivetti typewriter, he wrote long sincere thank-you letters for each book and donation, no matter how small.

He ended each letter with this message: "I assure you with my word and honor that this money has my paramount appreciation and will not be used for illegal purposes. Signed, Cordially Yours, James Bartholomew Bartlett, Polyhistor."

On Monday during our lunch hour, Papa and I met at Union Planters National Bank to open the first bank account he had ever had.

In his most businesslike voice, he said to the bank officer, "I have some money here, sir, and I would like to entrust it to your bank."

The bank officer looked at Papa for some time and said, "Have I met you before?"

"I don't believe so, but this bank holds the mortgage on my home, and I have made a payment on time every month for twenty-two years. Maybe you've seen me in the bank."

"No," he said, "it's something else. Are you that negro whose library burned down? I think I saw your picture in the paper. Did you actually read all those books?"

"Yes, sir, I did. I need to get back to work; can we get my account opened?" Papa asked.

"Sure. Peabody, right? You work at the Peabody?"

"Yes, and there's one more thing," Papa said and sat tall in his chair with his back straight. "I want to pay off my mortgage."

"That's quite an accomplishment for a negro. Congratulations."

With uncharacteristic irritation, he shot back at the bank officer, "Is your mortgage paid off?"

The man looked up from writing his forms. "I see you have a chip in your tooth. Did you get that from being a smart aleck?"

I stood up and faced the man. "I've got a chipped tooth too," I said and pointed to my front tooth. "Wanna make it three?"

With that the bank officer handed Papa the forms to sign, and as we left the bank, Papa had a broad smile as we walked into the sunshine of a cloudless, brilliant afternoon.

The day after I finished all the promised repairs on the house, Papa Jim and I laid a string outline on the ground of the new library we had been planning on paper every night after dinner. He went to bed, humming "The Old Rugged Cross." On Monday I began visiting supply stores to pick up the lumber and equipment I would need.

My efforts in rebuilding the library became a curiosity for the entire neighborhood. On Saturdays people stopped by to watch the progress from the porch. It lifted everyone's mood. Papa shared the growing number of pins on the map to wide-eyed guests and walked them through the house now filled with stacks and stacks of books.

Late one afternoon I looked down from the ladder to see a boy staring back up at me. I recognized him. He was the young man from the neighborhood I had seen from my bedroom window and the one in the crowd when the ladies brought Papa the books.

"Hello there," I said. "What's your name?'

His glasses were still held together with a Band-Aid, and he pushed them back on his nose and said, "I am Lucas Quentarious Ledbetter. They call me Lucky. I am Lucky Ledbetter. Who are you and what are you building here?"

"I'm Cotton Mathis, son. I'm building a new library for Mr. Bartlett."

"A library, huh? I am going to be in the third grade next year. Maybe you could read some of those books with me this summer."

I nodded and smiled at him. "Could you hand me that board from down there?"

"Sure," he said and handed the board up to me. "Could I help you? I can save you a lot of work handin' these boards up to you. Don't ya think?"

"I do, Lucky, and I think that's a great idea. How about if I pay you in ice cream?"

"We've got a deal," he answered.

We shook on it, and I put my hand on his shoulder. "About that name of yours, Lucky. Do you think you could spread some good fortune my way?"

"Well, that depends," he said, "on whether I like you or not. I haven't made my mind up about that yet."

After thinking about his response for a moment, I suggested, "How about if I ask your mom if it's okay for me to take you on Saturday to get your glasses fixed? Could I get in your good graces then?"

"Probably so," he said. "Since it is quittin' time, do ya think we could get some ice cream now?"

Sitting on the porch steps with our ice cream, I learned more about the Ledbetter family. His mother taught sixth-grade math at the neighborhood school. Lucky was an only child. When I asked about his father, he became animated.

"Right now my dad's in jail, but he's gettin' out on July eighth. That's not too many Saturdays from now."

I nodded. "No, son, that's not too long from now."

"He went in about the time I turned five, and I don't really remember much what he looks like. My mom gave me a picture, and I keep it in my shirt pocket all the time. I sleep with it at night too. I can't wait for him to get here. We're gonna play football together. D'you like football?"

"I do," I said. "My brother was a really good player in high school."

"Really? Well, my mom says my dad's a good man. He just got mixed up with bad people. He didn't know they were gonna steal a car, and he was tryin' to get out of there when the police came."

"Things go wrong sometimes, son."

"Yeah, I know, that's why I'm gonna grow up and be a lawyer...to help people like my dad."

As promised, the next Saturday I picked up Lucky early, and we rode the bus to an optometrist's office downtown. The lady who repaired the glasses was taken with Lucky.

"I don't often do this," she said, "but you are such a nice young man I'd like to give you a free eye test."

"No," said Lucky. "I can see fine with these glasses. I don't need that."

"Come on, Lucky," I said. "It won't take long. If you need new ones, I can help you with that."

"I don't want to."

"Come on, son, there's nothin' to it." I led Lucky to the large chair and plopped him down in it.

"Now," said the lady, "cover one eye and read the smallest letter you can see on the board."

Lucky covered his left eye. "I can't see anything," he said.

"You can't see anything? Don't you see this big letter right here?" she asked and pointed her stick at the huge E.

"No."

"Lucky, don't be rude. What's the matter with you?"

Lucky jumped from the chair, grabbed his glasses on the counter, and ran into the street.

"I am so sorry," I said to the lady and ran after him.

I found him sitting on the curb about a half block from the doctor's office. I sat next to him. "What is it, Lucky?"

"I can't...I can't read."

"What do you mean you can't read? Your mom's a teacher."

"She doesn't know, and I don't want her to know. She's had enough problems since my dad got sent away."

"How did you get sent up to the third grade then?"

"I cheat," he said.

"You cheat?"

"Yeah, it's better than worrying my mom about it. I don't know what I'm gonna do. If I tell the teacher, she's gonna tell my mom; they're friends."

"Come on," I said and picked him up by the shoulders. "Let's go back and work on the library. We'll figure this out."

CHAPTER TWENTY-EIGHT

When we got back to the house, Papa was waiting for me and Lucky to evaluate the progress on the Hippocrene. He started with, "I don't think that board is quite straight. Can you put a level on that to be sure? Let's leave a clean workplace—keeps people from getting hurt." He went on and on until I became distracted while using a hammer, missed the nail, and hit my thumb—hard.

"Dammit, that hurts. Could you give me a little peace and quiet here, Papa?"

"It looks like the nail split the wood; you might want to start over on that one," he answered.

Papa pulled a chair from the kitchen table and sat watching us with a book, *Proper Techniques for Do-It-Yourself Builders*. He read from it: "There is no substitute for doing the job right the first time. In the end, it will save amateur builders thousands in repair costs."

Lucky and I looked at one another and tried not to comment.

Later in the day, he would continue with, "You know the book says here there is a way to keep the floor from creaking. Come here and let me show you the pictures."

Lucky and I sat on the porch after a long day of listening to Papa and working on the library. "I think I have a plan to get you up to speed on your reading," I said.

Together we worked on a schedule that would make our secret reading mission possible.

Lucky gave up his afternoon playtime with his buddies to meet me before dinner, so I could help him with his reading skills and homework. On Saturdays we would work on reading over our ice cream.

We started on Monday and managed without his mother suspecting anything. She knew he spent his Saturdays helping me with the library, and her afternoons were spent grading papers at the school.

He moved through the alphabet and worked up to rudimentary reading. Lucky was an eager student and progressed well from the beginning.

"You know, Cotton, I was excited about the first grade, and then my dad got sent away, and it just got too hard."

"What about your mom—she didn't notice?"

"She cried every night for a year. I just got up every day and tried to make her laugh. I guess she had so much on her to take care of her students she forgot about me."

During my lunch hour the next day, I went to a stationery store downtown. I found a small journal there and gave it to Lucky that afternoon.

"This is for you to write down everything you are thinking about. It'll help you with your letters and sentences. You write all your secrets in there. It doesn't matter if you make mistakes at first; no one is going to read it but you."

Papa's books kept coming, along with letters, lots of them. Within a month there were volumes from every state and from twelve foreign countries.

Tipped off by one of Papa's friends at the Peabody, the newspaper reporter came back and interviewed him one afternoon. The next day an editorial appeared in the *Commercial Appeal*:

Memphis, Tennessee—A few months back we reported on the Negro man, James B. Bartlett, who lost his personal library, known as the Hippocrene, in a fire during the riots following the death of Dr. Martin Luther King in April. At the time Mr. Bartlett indicated he would not rebuild.

However, we are happy to report that partially because of our newspaper article, which was picked up by wire services worldwide, Mr. Bartlett has relented and with an associate of his, Mr. Cotton Mathis of Marianna, Arkansas, is rebuilding the library.

Mr. Bartlett has received hundreds of books from throughout the United States and foreign countries. Only a few of the donations have been from local patrons.

We at the Commercial Appeal would encourage our readers to respond to this outpouring of goodwill from around the world and get behind the efforts of this humble man who is trying to improve himself and his neighborhood. Our city needs healing, and there is no better salve than helping another in need.

Papa read the editorial aloud to me. When he finished, he said, "Seems to me they're doin' the same thing they did when Boaz got that medal. They put it on the front page of the paper just to try to convince themselves they're open-minded."

"What do you care? If they bring more books to you, what difference does it make?"

"I don't know. I guess I just don't believe this woulda happened if Dr. King hadn't been killed."

"Listen, Papa, we know now that no one in Memphis killed Dr. King. Let's give 'em the benefit of the doubt. There're people who feel just as bad as you do. Let's just wait and see what happens."

"What about you?" Papa asked. "Have you decided who you're gonna become after this library is finished?"

I didn't have an answer for him. I just escaped into the kitchen to start dinner and hoped he wouldn't ask again.

The next morning, as I placed the piece of cardboard over the mirror and began my shaving routine, Papa Jim came into the bathroom and ripped the cardboard from the mirror.

"That's enough of that," he said.

He replaced the cardboard with a note that he taped to the top of the mirror. It read,

Books cannot be killed by fire. People die, but books never die. No one and no force can abolish memory...In this war, we know, books are weapons. And it is a part of your dedication always to make them weapons for man's freedom.

—Franklin D. Roosevelt

In one of the cartons delivered by the mailman the day before, there was a copy of *Bartlett's Familiar Quotations*. I had the sinking feeling I was about to get schooled by Mr. Bartlett himself.

Lucky showed real promise in his reading. His mother was pleased he was spending so much time with us but never caught on to our real mission. He asked if he could speak with Papa one afternoon when we had finished our studies.

"My dad is coming home in two weeks. I really would like him to see the library. Do you think we could have a party for him here?"

"Sure, that would be just fine," Papa Jim said.

"Let's have cake," said Lucky, "and I know my dad would like barbecue. What about slaw and beans? My mom could make those. My uncle is gonna pick him up, and we'll all be waiting here to surprise him." When his mother called Lucky to dinner, there was a brightness in his eyes that I envied.

On the Saturday of the homecoming party, I rummaged through my sock drawer and found an unfamiliar piece of paper and opened it. On it was written the telephone number and name of the military-authority office where I could report my brother's murder. I had not thought about the note for a long time; I left it on the dresser and then, on second thought, stuck it in my pants pockets. Throughout the day I reached for it to make certain it was still in there.

Later in the morning, I caught myself being short with Papa Jim.

He said, "Hadn't thought about it before, but maybe I'd like running water in there, so I could wash up from the garden."

"You're making this so much harder," I said sharply. "This place was a shack before."

The words caught both of us off guard. I could see the deep hurt in his eyes, and it broke my heart. "I am so sorry. I didn't mean that," I said.

"It's all right," he said. "Just remember this library is more for your benefit than mine."

We both felt better later in the afternoon as we hung the decorations on the porch and Lucky's mom worked in the kitchen to prepare for the homecoming. The expected arrival was at four thirty.

At four o'clock, neighbors began to arrive, many of them bringing their own contributions to the festivities. Lucky had invited several friends from school, and they were tossing a football in the front yard.

Five o'clock came, and I could almost hear every tick of the clock as it reached six and early evening. Lucky's mother retreated to the house, and I found her crying in the back bedroom.

I tried to soothe her nerves. "They are just a little late; you know how the government is, nothing happens on time."

Lucky was undaunted. "He probably just stopped to see some old friends. Maybe he went to see the minister at our church. He'll be here soon."

The neighbors sensed there would be no celebration today and began to drift back home.

Finally, at six thirty, the uncle pulled up in his old sedan. "He's not coming. When I got to the prison gate, there was a woman there, and he left with her. I've been driving around looking for him all afternoon. I'm afraid he's gone for good."

I was sitting on the porch when the uncle delivered the terrible truth. Lucky careened across the yard and flew into my arms like a baby bird seeking shelter in a storm. His sobs were so violent that I was afraid he would be sick.

Papa Jim lifted him into the rocking chair and whispered in his ear: "Shhh now, boy, life ain't fair sometimes. You're learnin' that at an early age."

Lucky continued to cry and gulp. He tried to speak and was unable.

"Quiet now, times, important times like these, they deserve our silence. You need to try and not talk for a few days. Give yourself some time to heal from this. Silence is made of gold."

Lucky's mom took him gently from Papa's arms. We promised to visit them the next day and told them we would share the food with the neighbors.

Papa Jim retreated to the kitchen, and I stripped the decorations. Neither of us wanted to wake up in the morning to a reminder of this sad day.

I heard Papa call me from the house. "Cotton, hurry—there's a special report on the television."

A photograph of a man named James Earl Ray was being broadcast in living rooms throughout the nation. Spotted by a sharp-eyed Heathrow Airport immigration officer, he had been taken into custody earlier in the day. He was now on a flight to Memphis, where he would be charged with the assassination of Dr. Martin Luther King.

After Cronkite's report we made our way to the porch in silence. I stood and stared up at the moon from the porch for a long time; when I turned back around, Papa had already gone to bed.

As I undressed for bed, I reached into my pocket to put the key on the dresser, as was my habit. There was something else there: it was the piece of paper with the number of the military authorities.

I knew what I had to do. I went out into the yard and lifted the top off the trash can. Then I took the note and tore it into small pieces. As I tossed it inside, I thought of the garbagemen who would pick it up.

Hunting stories flooded through me as my bedroom desk and typewriter became my life rafts in a sea of sleeplessness. Finally, I sat in front of the Olivetti and I could not type fast enough to keep up with the torrent.

Two completed short stories emerged from that long night and, along with them, ideas for two more. In the morning the sun seemed brighter and the air crisper, and I felt more alive than I had felt in years.

That morning the quote on the bathroom mirror read,

Every burned book enlightens the world.

—Ralph Waldo Emerson

CHAPTER TWENTY-NINE

By the end of August, the Hippocrene would be finished. At the rate the books continued to come, there would be well over the number of original volumes.

Papa Jim sent Boaz a photograph of our progress and in his weekly letters described in detail the number of books donated and their origins. He still glowed when he spoke of the mortgage being paid off, and he wrote Boaz about it, leaving out the part about the rude bank officer.

Lucky, Papa, and I were stacking books one afternoon when the Christian ladies returned. This time they were not accompanied by an entourage.

The lawyer's wife knocked on the library door and said, "We read the library was being rebuilt, and we wanted to see it firsthand."

"Why, thank you, ladies. It has been a struggle to get it built properly with such inexperienced help, but I am fairly pleased with the results."

"If I may speak for the group, it's just lovely," she said. "Is there anything we could do to help?"

Papa Jim thought for a moment and said, "As a matter of fact, you see that young man there?"

"Yes."

"Well, he's become quite the reader, and since he is nine years old, I think he could handle some responsibility."

"What do you mean, Mr. Bartlett?"

"Our books are for adult readers. I am trying to talk this young fella into overseeing a lending library for the neighborhood kids, but we need some books children would like."

"Mr. Bartlett, you have put your trust in the right hands, hasn't he, ladies?" They all nodded in enthusiastic agreement. "We'll return with books in hand."

After soliciting their churches, the ladies appeared less than a month later with a large box of children's books and a promise for more to come in the future. Papa Jim, Lucky, and I drew plans for a small annex to the library, to serve as a lending office for the neighborhood.

The new note on the bathroom mirror read,

You can burn my books and the books of the best minds in Europe, but the ideas in them have seeped through a million channels, and will continue to quicken other minds.

—Helen Keller's response to Nazi book burning

For the first time in weeks, Lucky had an ear-to-ear smile under those glasses, just thinking about his job at the library.

"I can do it, Papa Jim. I promise I can do it," he said as we sat at the dining-room table sorting the books.

That afternoon after Lucky and I finished his reading lesson, he pointed to a photograph of Boaz over the fireplace. He was in full military dress and must have looked imposing to a nine-year-old boy.

"That's Papa Jim's son, isn't it?"

"Yes, he's in Vietnam."

"What's he like? Is he a good man?"

I thought about that for a moment and answered in the most positive way I could muster: "Papa's very proud of him. He's a war hero. He got a medal for saving three men."

"Wow!" Lucky said. "Do you like him?"

"Let me just say this, Lucky, if I was in the battle for my life, he would be the guy I would want next to me." I was surprised by my own answer.

That night I wrote in my journal what I had said to Lucky about Boaz, and I slept with it under my pillow. The next day I bought a magazine on book writing and from the back of it ordered a manual on finding a professional publisher. The articles had little encouragement for a first-time author, but I soldiered on with the writing.

There was rain Sunday night, so Monday morning was cooler than the usual mid ninety-degree summer in Memphis. I decided to get up early and walk to work.

Memphis looked different that morning. Changes not so obvious from the bus were evident in the city. Several businesses that had experienced heavy losses during the rioting now had Grand Reopening signs in their windows.

Workers planted flowers alongside the church where I had seen the man killed by the church bell. The repairs were finished, and the bell looked benign hanging in its tower.

There was a new bartender in The Green Beetle, and the place had a fresh coat of paint. Red-checked cloths covered the tables. The priest was nowhere in sight.

On the main retail streets of downtown, people greeted one another on their way to work. Schoolchildren on summer vacation looked in department-store windows with their mothers.

The movie theater was open, and people were already buying tickets for the day's early-bird special.

The Lorraine Motel had reopened. Just below and in view of where Dr. King had been shot, children were swimming in the pool. We even had three new long-term renters at the rooming house. The recent capture of James Earl Ray had given the city a breather, and Memphis was moving on with its life. Everyone now knew the man who killed Dr. King had not been among these people who prided themselves on being from the City of Good Abode.

There was another reason I wanted to walk that morning. I went by the Main Post Office and mailed ten of my stories to twenty publishers whose addresses I had found in the back of the literary magazine. Each one gave instructions to send at least fifty pages of writing and to wait for a response. They noted how few authors were selected by this process, but I knew I would never be published if I didn't mail them, so I sent hope on its way.

The rhythm of an ordinary Monday put a skip in my step, and the air was full of possibilities—until the spell was broken when the phone rang at three o'clock. A coworker of Papa Jim's called to report he had collapsed and was being taken by ambulance to St. Joseph's Hospital, where not long ago Dr. King had been pronounced dead.

The blood drained away from my face. I put the Closed sign at the front desk and raced to the hospital on foot. Papa Jim was being moved from a gurney to a bed in the emergency room when I arrived.

The attendant looked up from her stack of papers. "Are you Mr. Cotton Mathis?"

"Yes," I answered. "How did you know that?"

Papa called out, "Cotton, are you here, Cotton?"

He was groggy and confused. "I'm right here, Papa. We're going to get you taken care of," I assured him.

It was late afternoon before we were taken back to a room for the doctor to examine him. His blood pressure had dropped so low that he had fainted and would need to stay in the hospital for further tests.

I gave the nurse Boaz's unit number in Vietnam and the name of Papa's church. She assured me the hospital would notify the army and Papa's minister.

That night I slept on the chair close to his bed. The next morning he was somewhat better but still weak. "I have to go to work at least for a little while, Papa. I'll be back as soon as I can." He squeezed my hand.

All day I felt torn between the two places that needed my attention. While at the rooming house, I thought of nothing but the hospital. When I was at the hospital, I could not stop thinking about the rooming house. I closed the check-in desk early and sprinted to the hospital.

When I got to the room, Papa Jim's minister was there speaking with the nurse. He had often been at the house and had shown a real interest in the Hippocrene, even giving Papa Jim a special Bible to place there. He greeted me with a hug.

He said, "Jim's asleep right now. Why don't you and I go have a little talk outside. I know where there are a couple of benches and a fountain. Let's go downstairs."

Most ministers know when to go in for the kill, and I figured he thought I was so upset this would be the perfect moment to move me into the saved category. His church needed funds for a building project, and that too might be on his mind. Papa had shared with him the news that checks were sometimes included in the letters addressed to the library.

"No, I'd rather stay here with him. Thank you for coming to check on him." I tried to cut the minister off, hoping to avoid his solicitations.

"There'll be plenty of time for that. Come on now." He took me by the shoulder, and before I could argue, we were on the elevator going down. He pulled a handkerchief from his pocket and wiped sweat from his face. "Sure is hot today." It was the first time I noticed his nervousness.

Once we were seated, he said to me, "Son, I have some bad news for you. I don't know any other way but to just come out and say it. Papa Jim has cancer. It's in his stomach. He's known for almost eighteen months and refused treatment."

"What? He's been fine. You're mistaken; he would have told Boaz before he left."

"That's what I'm trying to tell you. He doesn't want Boaz to know. The doctors have been amazed he has managed to work and keep going for this long."

I felt sick. He certainly looked tired and older, but all of us in Memphis had suffered from the strain of the past few months. When Papa pushed the food on his plate around and didn't eat, I just thought he was upset about the assassination, Boaz's return to Vietnam, and the refusal of Lucky's father to come home. I had not given it much thought.

"Reverend, why are you telling *me* and not Boaz? Boaz should be here with his father. My mother died of cancer. I'm gonna be sick. I want out of here. I *can't* do this," I said.

He took my shoulder in a firmer way than I thought a minister should and said, "Cotton, you are a grown man now, and you need to reach down and find the best of yourself. They'll call Boaz in Vietnam, but the hospital has been instructed to play down the seriousness of it. Papa will speak with you about that. It's you he wants to take care of him."

"But how am I going to take care of him once he gets home?" I said.

Then came the worst of the news. "Cotton, I don't think you need to worry about bringing him home. He came by my office a couple of weeks ago and brought an updated last will and testament. You're listed in those papers as the only person allowed to speak with the doctor about his condition."

"Me—why me?" I asked.

"You go on back upstairs, and he'll tell you. I'll come by and check on him every day."

My steps were so heavy it took a long time to get to the elevator and longer to walk down the hall to Papa Jim's room. I put my hand on the door, and I was overwhelmed with grief. I cried for all of them: my parents, my brother, and Papa. I found a bench in the hallway to collect myself before going in the room. The nurse brought me a towel and suggested I go wash my face before going in. I did as told and steeled myself for what was ahead of me.

The light was streaming through the window; it lit Papa Jim up in an ethereal way when I returned. There was an elegance in his bone structure I had never noticed; he was thin and weak. His long fingers were clasped together on top of the blanket.

"You've spoken with the reverend?" he asked.

I didn't reply; instead, I just knelt next to the bed and wept on his stomach with his beautiful hands now resting on my head. I sobbed until there was nothing left.

"That's enough of that now, Cotton. Sit down, and let me talk with you. I need to go over some things before this medicine puts me back to sleep."

He spoke in a deliberate manner. "Now, you listen to me. I was in World War II, and I know what war takes out of a man. Vietnam is so much worse. Our own people are against us, and the government won't let us win it."

"I know, Papa, I know," I said.

"I don't want Boaz worried about me; he could get himself killed or hurt. This country is gonna do somethin' about civil rights, and I want my son to live to enjoy that."

"I hear what you are saying, but I just don't feel right about it."

"The military will pay for his college, Cotton. Boaz will be the first person to ever go to college in my family, and he's promised he'll graduate. I want my boy to come back whole. I want him to get a *real* education, not like mine."

"I'll do it, Papa—I'll do anything to help you through this," I said.

He drifted to sleep, and I left to take care of the rooming-house business. There was a long-term renter who I thought could help me through the next few weeks. We worked out a deal that I would be there in the mornings and she would come take my place at the front desk about noon each day. She would stay throughout the evening and be available for any problems that might arise.

The next stop was the school, where I told Lucky's mother that Papa Jim would be in the hospital for a while, and she agreed to get the mail, bring me the bills, and water the garden. She would let our neighbors know, so they could keep an eye on things during the day. I got my clothes and the things I would need for several days. On the way back to the hospital, I dropped by the Peabody and told the manager Papa would be out for a while. He said that after all these years of service, Papa would still receive his paycheck until he felt well enough to come back to work. I began my hospital vigil that night.

With rest and the Boaz issue resolved, Papa got a little stronger and even began to eat. The doctor said he was doing as well as could be expected.

In the afternoons he was more lucid and enjoyed visiting. We talked until dinnertime and went to sleep early. Once I became accustomed to the hospital cot, I slept well and often got to the rooming house before sunrise.

We had long conversations about neighborhood gossip and Memphis news. One afternoon I inquired about Papa Jim's family and upbringing.

I grew up in Sugar Ditch, near Tunica, Mississippi," he said. "It was one of the poorest counties in this country, but we didn't know that. I loved it there."

"I know what you mean, Papa; I feel that way about Arkansas too."

"That flat, jet-black Delta land stretches all the way to the river. In the summer when the sun sets, we used to call it 'the pinkness,' because that big ole sun drops into the river and the sky goes pink," he said.

"It sounds beautiful."

"You know, Cotton, I'm the only one left in my family, like you."

"Really? What happened to them, Papa?"

"My parents were sharecroppers, and they just wore out. Daddy died of a heatstroke one August, and Mama just gave up after that."

"You had brothers and sisters?"

"I was the youngest of four. My brother died of a botched aneurysm surgery when he was in the service. One sister died of breast cancer, and the other of lung cancer. We used to have family reunions at the homestead every year. I miss my family."

After the first day of listening to him reminisce, I bought a notebook and wrote down everything he said to make a diary of his hospital stay, starting from the first day he was taken to the emergency room.

Every afternoon he talked and I wrote. "I met Emmaline at the Baptist Church when we were eleven years old. We got married when we were seventeen. She had three miscarriages after she had Boaz, so we just quit tryin'," he said.

He drifted in and out of sleep. "My brother loved the farm, so after our parents died, he stayed home to work the place. Emmaline and I were part of the first wave of our people who came up from the Delta. She worked for the same family for thirty-eight years."

"You liked your job, Papa?"

"I loved working at the Peabody," he answered. "I've waited on people from all over the world. It's been part of my education."

Looking back now, I realize those afternoons with Papa Jim gave a gentleness to my life I had never known. Often as I wrote in that notebook, I had to wipe away tears.

He continued, "Have I ever told you about the war?"

"No, please, I want to hear about it," I said.

"I was in the Seven Hundred Sixty-First Tank Battalion. You know, black people weren't allowed to serve with white people. We were called the Black Panthers. We were mainly boys from the South...our motto was Come Out Fighting. We were tough."

"I'll bet you were." I laughed. I had read about the famous 761st. Their bravery and contributions to the war were legendary.

He continued, "We were in some dicey situations during the war, but we held our own in all of them. General Patton gave us a special assignment to guard warehouses during the Battle of the Bulge. I'm so proud I served with those men. I knew Jackie Robinson; we were friends at Fort Hood."

"What? You mean *the* Jackie Robinson, Papa?" I thought the medication must be playing tricks on his mind.

"That's the one," he said. "He got out of the Seven Hundred Sixty-First on trumped-up charges, and he never got to go overseas. We kept in touch for a long time. When the Brooklyn Dodgers played in the 1955 World Series, a friend and I took the train all the way from Memphis to New York City just to see one game. Jackie got us tickets."

"That is an amazing story, Papa. Does Boaz know about that?"

"I don't know if he remembers; he was young when I made the trip. I got to go to the New York Public Library. You should see the big granite lions outside the building. I think that is my favorite place on earth. It's so grand, I just know it is what heaven is gonna be like."

"You look tired," I said, but he was already asleep. I flipped the cover over the notebook, walked down the long hospital hall, and looked out the window at the end of the building. A gorgeous summer sunset was on display, with neon-pink colors peeking through the clouds.

CHAPTER THIRTY

One week turned into two and then three at the hospital. Papa was losing his battle to cancer. He was weak. The afternoons became quieter. The hospital-diary notebook was filled with gems of wisdom, and I turned back to my short stories. I tried not to think about the publishers who had not yet responded to me and kept busy writing notes and phrases for story ideas. Books from the Hippocrene helped me to fall asleep, and the characters from them populated my dreams.

Boaz kept in touch with the minister and called as often as he was able. He was assured that Papa was coming along and would be glad to hear his son had called. Papa always perked up when the reverend came to visit with news from Boaz.

One afternoon Papa woke from his medicated sleep and called out, "Cotton...Cotton, are you there?"

"Yes, I'm right here," I said.

"Is the library finished? Did we finish it?"

"It sure is; we just need to do a few more things to the lending office. You know, we still get a few books in the mail every week."

"I want to see it one more time, Cotton. I want to see my Hippocrene one more time."

I sat there a long while, holding my thumbnail between my teeth and trying to come up with the right answer.

"Cotton, did you hear me?" he said. "I want to see the Hippocrene just once more."

"I heard you, Papa. I promise I'll do what I can to get you there."

The next afternoon I left the minister at the hospital to go back to the house. I needed clean clothes and wanted more books to read over the coming weekend, and I had an idea.

I picked up the phone and called back home to Arkansas. "Booker, you and Sallie and Dew all right?"

"Sure, Cotton," he said in his deep, rich voice.

"Booker, I need your help with something."

"Sure, whatever you need. I read about Mr. Bartlett in the *Commercial Appeal*; what are ya doin' buildin' a library for?"

I went over my plan with Booker and then went by the school to find Lucky's mother grading papers. I would need her help too for my plan.

I left her classroom feeling as though we might just be able to make Papa's wish a reality.

Lucky was outside in the schoolyard playing touch football with his neighborhood friends. There was a white child with them, which was curious, as it was not often white children were seen in this neighborhood.

The boys were bent over, looking for something on the ground, when I walked out of the school. In the hot, humid afternoon, a thunderstorm brewed on the horizon. A pocket of cold air hit me as I walked across the field. My brother had taught me that cold air signals a drastic change coming in summer weather patterns. I should get the boys to move inside, as lightning was now flashing in the distance.

"What are you looking for, fellas?" I asked.

The white child looked at me and said, "My compass. It musta dropped outta my pocket. I have to find it. My dad gave it to me."

The hair on my head stood up as though from the electrical charge in the lightning. And then I saw it. "Son, is your front tooth chipped?"

"Yeah, I got it playing football. Why?"

"No reason," I answered. "I have one too." I pointed to my mouth, and the boy peered into it.

Lucky spotted something on the ground. "Here it is, Jack, right here." He handed the prized compass to the boy.

Again the cold air swept around me. "Is that your name... Jack?"

"Yes sir, I'm Jackson, but they call me Jack. I'm named after my dad," he said.

I spoke slowly, "My brother's name was Jackson, and he had a compass. He never let me use it." I could see the boys leaning in to hear me. I was almost speaking in a whisper. "Your dad must be proud of you, son."

"Yes, sir, he was, but he died in Vietnam two months ago. My mom and I, we just moved here from Columbus, Ohio. We needed a new start. She's going to be a teacher in this school."

All chatter in my mind ceased. I tried not to let the astonishment of what he said register on my face. This young man holding a compass, speaking to me through his chipped tooth with the same name as my brother, was traveling the same path of sorrow I had traversed.

"My brother died several years ago in Vietnam. He never had the opportunity to get married and have a son. I am so sorry for what you and your mother have been through. No one knows how it feels until it happens in their family."

From behind me came a gentle breeze of a voice from the most appealing woman I had ever seen. "My name is Evie. I see you've met my son, Jack."

She had long auburn hair and green eyes. Against her, the sky glowed, framing her in light. The storm had passed around us. The sky was opening up to light rays bursting through the clouds. Evie was becoming uncomfortable as I stared at her a little too long. My attention was diverted only by Lucky giving me two thumbs up from behind her.

The boys were ready to go back to their game, and I made small talk with Evie while they tossed the football back and forth. She called for Jack to come along for supper. Lucky waved good-bye to his new friend and headed across the field for home. I watched him as he sauntered away, and then he turned, looked at me, and gave a deep bow like a performer who had received a standing ovation.

The next day I spoke with the doctor and told him my plan for Papa to come to the Hippocrene one more time. The doctor said that if we could get him stronger in a week, Papa could make the trip home, so that afternoon I went by the Peabody to enlist the help of the staff there with our plans.

Finally, I was able to tell Papa about the celebration we were planning. His eyes shone with tears as I said, "Now you have to work hard the next several days. You have to get strong enough for the doctor to let us go."

He began to eat everything on his plate and asked me to bring him ice cream when I came to the hospital after work.

"The library's finished, and we're going to have a big party," he told Boaz by phone. "I'll send you pictures."

Saturday was a glorious, cloudless day. Lucky's uncle came to the hospital with me, and we put his wheelchair in the back of his car.

Papa said, "I feel like a kid at Christmas."

When we got to the house, I was so busy trying to get Papa out of the car and into the wheelchair I didn't see what was happening in the front yard. Lucky's mother and the neighbors had decorated for a full-scale celebration. There were balloons everywhere, children played in front of the library office, and choir members from Papa's church sang on the front porch.

The newspaper reporter was there with his camera, and he was talking with Papa's friends from the Peabody. The neighbors came to greet us at the sidewalk, and they helped me lift the wheelchair up the steps.

Lucky waved me over to come look at something. He was with Jack, and then I saw the large cream-colored dog. It was Dewdrop. He leapt at me with all four legs off the ground and wrapped his paws around my neck, licking my face and head with joy.

The smell of barbecue took me right back home, and there was Booker with Sallie cooking in the side yard. I raced for him and threw my arms around him, with Dew right behind me.

"Man, do you two look great! I have never been so glad to see two people."

"You don't look so bad yourself there, Cotton. Sallie and I couldn't wait to get here. Dew has been waiting by the truck for two days. I think he knew we were coming to see you. That library is beautiful." Sallie held my arm tight as Booker spoke.

The sound of familiar laughter came from across the yard. There were Froggie and Timbo pointing to my truck from home, and it was waxed and shining. I was overcome with tears as they all gathered around me. For the first time in years, I felt like I was surrounded by family.

"Papa, these are the people who helped me all my life. Could we show them the Hippocrene together?" He put his hand on mine and nodded.

The minister was there, and with him were the ladies and the yardman who had brought Papa the books.

But the biggest surprise of the day was when a tall, white man emerged from a car parked just down the street. He walked over to us and extended his hand to Papa. "Hello, sir, I'm the former mayor of Memphis. I heard about the party from these church friends," he said as he pointed to the ladies. "I hope you don't mind if I came."

Before he could finish, Papa said, "Yes, Mayor Orgill. Edmund Orgill, I am so happy to see you again. I waited on you often at the Peabody, sir. Do you remember the time I dropped the tray and you helped me pick up all those dishes?"

"That seems like a long time ago now; so much has happened. I just want you to know the whole city has been lifted by your story," Orgill replied.

I wheeled Papa to the entrance of the Hippocrene, and he said, "I'm going to walk inside."

It took a monumental effort for him to stand, but I helped, and together we entered the library. He stood there, as I had the first time, and slowly circled the room. Tears were running down both our faces. "I am...I *am*," he said with emotion, "so pleased, Cotton."

By late afternoon Papa became tired and weak. "Cotton, can I spend a few minutes alone in my house; won't take but a minute," he said.

With help, I lifted his wheelchair up the front porch steps and set him in the middle of the house, so he could see most of it. "I'll be back in a few minutes to get you." He squeezed my hand and nodded.

After a while I knocked gently on the doorsill, and he motioned for me to come in. "We were so happy here. I loved every day I lived in this house. It makes me so happy to know that Boaz will live here. I know where I belong now; let's go."

Back at the hospital, we got him settled into his room. He refused dinner and went right to sleep. "I'll be back after I grab a little dinner; I want to get there before the cafeteria closes," I told the nurse.

When I returned from supper, I saw the doctors, nurses, and equipment at the end of the hallway. I ran to Papa Jim's room. The minister was there. "I'm glad you got back; it's almost time. I'm so grateful I thought to come check on him after the party. I want to make sure he has a painless passage to Home."

I asked all of them to leave, and I tried not to give into my wobbling knees. I knelt next to his bed. I could see the veins of Papa's hands through his skin. He was so weak. Labored breathing made the top of his chest heave and collapse with a soft wheezing sound.

"Not yet, Papa, not yet...wait and let us call Boaz."

Then Papa squeezed my hand and tried to respond. He could only manage to whisper and said, "Cotton, my job was always to get you home. You can make it the rest of the way without me. Just please find a way in your heart to forgive Boaz."

I draped my body on top of Papa and sobbed. "I did forgive him, Papa; I tore up the note."

But he was already gone. His chest was no longer heaving, and a profound peace emanated from his face. It was so different than the faces of my dead father and brother. It was the face of a man fully at peace with his life.

The nurse and doctor came back into the room to check his vital signs. The nurse shook her head at me, and the doctor told her to mark the time of death in her records. The minister was behind them, and he lifted me from Papa's chest.

He said, "Come on now, Cotton; it's all over. I need to call Boaz."

I trudged back home to Papa's and stayed awake all night, writing about every detail of the day: the ride from the hospital, the library celebration, and Papa's final hours.

I slept late and had lunch on the front porch. Neighbors came by with condolences and food to ask about the arrangements that would be made when Boaz got home. The phone rang as I made my way back to the kitchen to clean up my plate. It was Boaz.

"Listen, you son of a bitch," he said. "I want you out of that house, and *now*! Do you understand me? You destroyed what my father spent his life building, and now you've taken his last days from me. You're not welcome at the funeral. You are *just as evil* as your *brother.*"

Before I could respond, he slammed down the phone. Panic rose in my gut. I stuffed my belongings into a box, turned the light off, placed the hospital diary on the dining-room table, and locked the front door behind me.

I no longer belonged here. I could go back to the rooming house and wait the few days until Miss Bessie returned, and then I would go home to Arkansas.

Since my brother and father's deaths, my life had been a tight spool of thread wound round and round. Every day since meeting Boaz, the thread had become more unspooled, and I was now an unsewn mess on the floor. Papa was the only person who had helped me rethread the needle of redemption, and now he was gone.

CHAPTER THIRTY-ONE

Lying on the bed in the rooming house, I cried late into the night for Papa. I thought a drink might help and reached for my wallet to go find a bar still open at this hour. I tucked in my shirt and went to the sink to wash up.

Drying my face, I caught my reflection in the mirror. I thought of a quotation Papa had left for me one morning:

You have not converted a man just because you have silenced him.

—John Morley

My thoughts turned to Evie, and I prayed I would see her again. She was not the kind of girl who might be interested in a drunk. I resisted the idea of going to the bar and lay on the bed hoping I would dream of her.

Neglected chores at the rooming house kept me busy. I wanted everything to be clean and in order when Miss Bessie returned and was thankful for the distraction.

The day before she was due home, I walked from the rooming house onto the sidewalk as I wiped paint thinner from my hands with a rag. I squinted against the light to see someone waving at me from the park bench across the street.

It was Lucky, and he was holding the hand of a man who was wearing a military uniform. It was Boaz, and he shook my hand and then wrapped both arms around me in a long hug. "I spoke with the minister," he said. "I know now why you didn't tell me about the cancer."

I looked down to hold back tears and nodded, overwhelmed with relief.

"I read the notebook," he continued. "I'll always be grateful."

"Papa just wanted you to come home safe, Boaz," I said.

"I know," he said, "and I'll be home for good in a couple of months. Lucky and his mom have agreed to take care of the house and the Hippocrene until I get back."

"Boaz, I'm going back home…back home to Arkansas."

"That's good," he said, "but first, would you sit with me at Papa's funeral?"

The church was crammed with mourners, both black and white. Papa Jim had been a member of this congregation for forty-two years. The energetic choir sang songs of redemption in Papa's honor. The minister opened his address by saying there was no finer example of what it means to be "I AM A MAN" than James Bartholomew Bartlett.

The Christian ladies were there, too, and were particularly moved by the choir. They danced in the aisles with a passion that would have shocked their own congregations. After the service, the lawyer's wife told Boaz his father had been an inspiration for all of Memphis at a time when the community needed it most. The newspaper reiterated her comments and more in an obituary and report of the funeral the next day.

When Boaz and I arrived back at the house, the neighbors had prepared a feast of casseroles, homemade breads, and desserts. Vases of fresh flowers filled the house. Papa Jim's friends from the Peabody Hotel were there, along with other friends and church members. Boaz received well-wishers until late in the afternoon.

I was recruited into the kitchen to dry dishes, and I heard Boaz speak in the dining room with someone whose voice was familiar. I looked through the door to see Lucky's mother. She was not alone. Evie and Jack stood next to her.

Jack looked up at Boaz and gave him a military salute. When Evie looked my way, she stifled a laugh with her hand to her mouth. I was wearing an apron and drying my hands with a kitchen towel.

She said, "Look at you there in your ruffled apron—nice look."

I smiled back at her.

She continued, "Lucky's mom told me all about Papa Jim. She also told me about the time you spent with Lucky and how he tricked you into believing he couldn't read, even though he is the strongest reader in his class."

All I could do was laugh. "You mean to tell me that kid could read all along? He is something else."

"He just needed some male attention, and you were there. It was really kind of you." She smiled.

"Do you think we could see a movie and have the dinner next week?" I asked.

She smiled. "I'd look forward to that, but you don't need to wear your apron."

After we finished in the kitchen and the last of the mourners had gone home, Boaz said, "Lucky, could I get you and your mom to sit with me and Cotton for just a few minutes before you leave? A couple of days ago, the minister brought some papers for me to go over. My dad's last wishes were in there, and part of that concerns the two of you. Papa wrote to me about you all the time. He was quite smitten with you, young man."

Lucky looked over, shrugged, and smiled at his mother.

"There's a good amount of money in Papa's bank account. Cotton, did he ever tell you how much people had sent him?"

"No. I had no idea."

"Yes, there's enough to take care of the house and library for a long, long time, but even better, he left Lucky twenty-five thousand dollars to pay for college and law school—all the expenses."

This news so overwhelmed Lucky's mother that she grabbed her son and cried into his small shoulder.

When he ran to me, I took Lucky by the shoulders and said with a wink, "And to think when you got here, you couldn't even read, huh?"

He said to all of us, "I always knew there was a reason my dad gave me this nickname. It's because I am the luckiest boy on earth."

CHAPTER THIRTY-TWO

B oaz was exhausted. I sent him to bed, saying, "You are going to sleep really well in your own bed tonight. I'll be back late morning to give you plenty of time to rest. We can finish cleaning up then."

The lights in the Hippocrene shone through the new windows, and I thought of the first time I had seen it, with the wood stove burning and the gas lamp on the arm of the chair. I stood in the middle of the modest building Lucky and I had constructed, and I ran my hand over the neat rows of shelves, so unlike the tumble and jumble of the original library.

The memories swept through me. I saw the first time I met Boaz and his intimidating presence, our work for the police force, and my daily drinking habit.

I remembered learning the truth about my brother and the brutal consequences of his behavior. I thought of my runaway anger and my attack on Boaz. I relived the assassination and pictured the men pointing up toward the rooming house in the direction of the killer. I thought of the riots and uneasiness in Memphis that followed. But the most vivid memory was of myself lighting the match and setting the Hippocrene afire. Even now, it was unbearable to think about.

I heard Papa Jim speaking his illuminations on guilt, silence, and redemption. I pictured him in uniform standing next to an army tank with Jackie Robinson. Finally, I saw him in the hospital and me next to him, writing down his memories.

Papa Jim had refused to die until great good had been harvested from this field of woe. I picked up a book and flipped through its pages; a note in Papa's handwriting fell to the floor. It was dated, April 4, 1968, the day Dr. King was assassinated; it read,

Evil is swift of foot as it travels through alleyways with few obstacles. But Right, now that is a different story. Right rides a wagon of wooden wheels whose horses falter through every pothole and bulge in the road. When its destination is reached, Evil is refreshed and ready for dinner with friends; Right arrives ragged and torn, a compromise of its original form. Right pleases no one in the end but still manages somehow to make better everyone's lives.

—James "Papa Jim" Bartholomew Bartlett

When I got back to the rooming house, a letter waited for me. Its return address was Random House Publishing, New

York, New York. The letter would change the trajectory of my life.

The day the cartons of my own book arrived at my doorstep, I threw them open and thought of the first box of books that had come from Massachusetts to restock the Hippocrene after the fire. That night I slept with one of my volumes in the bed next to me. My book would be in stores by Saturday, and Evie, Jack, Lucky, and I were going to see them on the shelves.

I picked up the three of them that morning and treated them to a pancake breakfast. Evie said in her soft way, "Papa Jim would be so pleased for you, Cotton."

Over seventy-five people were waiting when I arrived at the bookstore. There on a table at the entrance were a stack of my books and my photograph, with a copy of the nice review the *Commercial Appeal* had written about the book. There were quotes from me about Papa Jim and the profound influence he had had on my writing.

The four of us watched as a young man flipped through my book, lowered himself to the floor, and began to read the first chapter with his back against a bookshelf. Lucky moved toward the boy to tell him I was the book's author. With my finger to my mouth, I shook my head. I wanted to watch the boy's reaction. He turned to ask his mother if he could buy the book, and she nodded.

AFTER

I have eight books in print now and continue to work full-time as a writer. I still write about hunting and fishing, with the hope of giving young people a sense of responsibility toward the creatures and their habitat, with which we have been entrusted.

Dr. Martin Luther King has become the iconic figure of the American civil-rights movement, with buildings, bridges, and highways named in his memory. But this was never his intention for his life. He would have been content being a minister to his own Atlanta flock.

An idea may be slow in coming to this country, but when its time arrives, it can happen at a breakneck speed, which sweeps up innocents in its ambitions. When the collective vision of righteous people collides, change is inevitable. The lowly garbagemen of Memphis had that vision. Their place in civil-rights history is secure. We live in an imperfect world, where mistrust persists on all sides of the civil-rights issues. But there is evidence of progress all around us.

Change is never welcome by everyone in a democracy. In 1963 Dr. King led his triumphant March on Washington, gave his "I Have a Dream" speech, and met with a supportive President John F. Kennedy, who in a short time would be assassinated in Dallas. Ironically, after King was murdered in April 1968, Robert Kennedy would be assassinated that June. King's life was bookended by both Kennedy deaths.

The city of Memphis and the nation continue to strive for the hopeful images of racial understanding described by the idealistic young Dr. King, who died there in 1968 at the age of thirty-nine. The next year, America fulfilled Kennedy's promise to win the space race against the Soviets when Neil Armstrong became the first man to walk on the moon. The five hundred million people worldwide who watched from their television sets on Earth included many Americans who hoped the worst was behind us and our future would be bright.

It took me a few years to understand I had a responsibility to be aware of the cultural, social, and political issues around me. Looking back now, I see I was so trapped in a vise of self-pity that even when Dr. King died before my eyes, all I could think of were my own tragedies. In the end, I am indebted to him. No one's life was more changed than mine by his presence in Memphis, Tennessee, in the spring of 1968.

James Earl Ray pleaded guilty to the assassination of Dr. King and was sentenced to ninety-nine years in prison. In 1977 he escaped with six other convicts and was captured three days later. He died in prison of hepatitis C.

The connections in our lives entwine us, bind us, and align us. They are everywhere. From the miracle of our birth through our parents, to our deaths from causes like genetics and environment, we are at the mercy of our connections.

I have come to realize that God's task for us is that we negotiate our way through the complex relationships present in our surroundings. None of us asks to be born, and certainly if we had a choice, many of us would not have chosen to be placed in the family selected for us. But he gives us free will to negotiate the connections in our lives in a multitude of ways that determine our own fate.

Boaz and I have a connection. We are close, and we are grateful for the slow peeling away of the scabs of our past, so we might heal one another. Our connection through Papa Jim was a gift from a man who was a statistical exception in the universe. Papa's connections weren't with people but with the whole of humanity, which is a rare gift to hold and to witness. Anyone who has the fortune to be cast in that light is made better for the connection. All of us who loved him and the Hippocrene Library he left behind have thrived.

Boaz came home from the war. He finished college and now works for an accounting firm. Soon after coming back to Memphis, he started dating Lucky's mother, and they are married now. Boaz proved to be a natural at fatherhood. Lucky was successful in his studies and fulfilled his law-school dream.

I have a family now too. In time, Evie was persuaded to marry me, and she and Jack love Arkansas just as I do. She is still a teacher, and one beloved by her students. I write full-time, and my books have been well received, with a larger audience than I could have ever imagined. I have a son of my own. His name is James Booker Mathis. He calls me Papa. I call him Jim.

Jack became a son to me, just as if he were my own. He's now a young man with a wife and family, graduated from agricultural college and farming his own land.

Not long ago we sat together on the back porch on a crisp, bright November day, cleaning our guns for the hunting-season opener.

"Dad," said Jack, "I was thinking yesterday: you always told me your brother taught you everything you know about the woods, but you never told me much about him. What was he like?"

"You know, son, it's funny you would ask. He's been on my mind for months now. I just finished writing a book about him. I haven't decided yet whether I'm going to have it published."

"Why?" he asked.

I rose from my chair and retrieved the manuscript from my office. "I'll read a little of it to you, and then we'll talk about it."

I settled back in my chair and began to read my own words: "On a Friday just before noon, my brother and I, dog-tired from the Indian-summer heat, made our way through thick woods. For over an hour, I had been out of water, but my brother, still with a half-full canteen, was determined not to leave until he had killed a deer."

I looked up from the page and into the woods, remembering it all.

"Dad, you all right?" Jack asked.

"Yeah, son, I'm fine. This can wait for another day. Tell you what, I'm going to put this manuscript in the lockbox. Promise me you'll send it to my publisher after I'm gone."

"What do you mean? You're not going anywhere."

"Please," I put on hand on his shoulder, "remember this conversation, and do what I ask."

"Sure, yes, sir, I'll do it first thing; I won't forget when the time comes." Jack assured me.

"Let's go load the truck, and tomorrow we're gonna get a big buck. I can feel it in my bones. We're not gonna leave the woods until we have us a big buck."

Later I cut a piece of cardboard to protect the manuscript and to cover the words, which formed sentences representing the ideas, the places, and the people who populated my past, and I placed it in the safety of the lockbox—in the darkness and silence where they all belonged.

The End

ACKNOWLEDGMENTS

In closing, I have such gratitude to the great Otis Sanford who reminded me that writing is so much fun, far more fun than anything else. I want to thank him and Suzanne Kerr for that and for allowing me to be part of their great team of writers for a short time at the *Memphis Commercial Appeal.*

This book began on a porch overlooking Lake Androscoggin in Maine at the idyllic camp of Jim and Beth Breazeale. Without their constant encouragement and that of our friend Jann Gilmore, I would not be writing these final words today.

At the end of this project, I had the good fortune to meet and be helped by best-selling author Curtis Wilkie whose blending of newspaper-reporting skills and storytelling bring wonder to every word he writes.

Finally, I owe someone I never had the privilege to meet. Joan Turner Beifuss's book *At the River I Stand,* though long out of print, is a fine narrative whose words still leap from the page. The three times I read this book before sitting down to my computer to write convinced me there are still many books waiting to be written about Memphis.

ABOUT THE AUTHOR

News reporter Cecilia Croft Clanton grew up near Memphis and witnessed the aftermath of Martin Luther King Jr.'s assassination firsthand.

Clanton has written for the *Springdale News*, the *Arkansas Gazette*, and the *Memphis Commercial Appeal*. In addition, she has experience in the corporate business world and motion-picture industry. She now lives on a Mississippi farm, where she spends time in her oil-painting studio, minding her chickens and writing.